DANCE
of the
HANGED
MAN

Mark Greene

Dedicated to my son, who tells such fine stories.

Dance of the Hanged Man
Published by ThinkPlay Partners
ISBN: 979-8-9870246-2-1
©2023 by Mark Greene
All Rights Reserved

Table of Contents

Chapter 1: Tree House

The summer of 1974 was hot. Across the vast sprawl of Houston, the temperature remained in the 90's well past sundown, leaving the laundry hanging limp on the lines; slow to dry in the humid night air. By July, even the children who had grown up running barefoot down the white-hot sidewalks would creep inside after lunch to wait out the heat of early afternoon; reemerging to wander along the fence lines and tumble through the front yards, their scuffed knees damp and itchy with grass stains and sweat.

A boy climbed up into the limbs of a towering sycamore tree. Afternoon sunlight drifted down in hazy shafts through the canopy of green leaves. Cicadas droned among the winding limbs. Empty yards spread out below, silent in the glare of the hot sun. Wiping sweat from his eyes, he struggled to lift a long pine board. The trees in neighboring yards about him were utterly still in the shimmering heat, waiting patiently for a breeze to stir their leaves into languid motion. A car horn honked in the distance.

He talked to himself as he wrestled the board into place and began hammering nails. His left eye ticked convulsively. He set his jaw and pounded away with fierce determination. Sweat drifted down along his nose. He looked warily toward the back door of the distant house. He glanced up through the dazzling green leaves, addressing the empty branches above. "She'll be out here any minute," he said loudly. "You just wait."

He had just turned fourteen the previous month, June. He was already awkwardly tall and lanky, his bristly hair cut short in a burr. His caste and complexion were dark, except for his eyes, which were a bright shocking blue. He had a hooked nose and thin lips, which were turned down in a scowl. His narrow hawkish features were out of place on a boy his age, but then, nothing about James was quite normal. The nail he was hammering bent. He straightened it and drove it home.

Somewhere down among the empty yards, a dog began barking in the shimmering heat, alarmed by the noise. But the barking soon faltered and fell silent. James studied his handiwork. The board had not split, despite the size of the nails he was using. He lifted himself and shifted his weight onto the board.

"What are you doing, James?"

He was startled by his mother's voice. She stood at the base of the tree looking up at him. Her arms jutted out from the sleeves of her dress. She was all elbows and knuckles, pale hard angles.

"I want you down from this tree. It's not safe," she said.

"There's nothin' wrong with this tree…" he said, half under his breath, glaring at her angrily. He felt his skin flush.

"I said get down," she replied flatly.

"It's just a treehouse…," James' argument trailed off.

She continued to stare at him, impatient. The urge to stand his ground came in waves, like surf on the beach. He drew himself up.

His mother took a step back so as not to have to look straight up at him. She shaded her eyes with one hand. "Just come down here."

James stared at the woman below. *Go back in your stupid house,* he thought bitterly. Her features darkened. He watched the play of emotions across her face. So far, there were only small indications of her irritation. He knew that every second he delayed risked far worse. Trembling, he made no move to climb down. His jaw became set, drawing his mouth into a thin line.

"This is the last time I'm gonna ask you," she said, her voice deceptively calm.

James felt a giddy hysteria blend with his anger. A sense of anticipation grew in him. He glanced up though the leaves. "I'll come down when I'm good and ready."

She stepped up, planting one foot on a thick root, and clambered part way up into the tree. She was rising toward him, an awkward and spindly shape against the bright green grass below. Before he knew it, she was much too close. The skin around her eyes was rigid and trembling. She took hold of his ankle. Her grip was firm. James scrambled to steady himself.

"So help me God, I'll yank you out of this tree," she said between her teeth.

James struggled to regain his balance. His mother's grip was growing painfully tight, her volatile temper creating immense strength. All rebelliousness drained out of him. He gripped a narrow branch above his head and shifted his weight, steadying himself on the board. The hammer tumbled off, falling end over end toward the ground, landing with a thump.

"Momma!" he said, growing alarmed.

"Get...down," she hissed. Her foot slipped and her free hand scrabbled claw-like for a purchase on a nearby branch. Her thin arms became ropy with twisting muscles as she pulled herself higher into the tree. The skin on her face was rigid; drained of color. An unnatural twitching erupted in the flesh below one eye; as if a worm was writhing just below the skin, turning over and over. Her grip became stronger, her nails biting into his bare leg, grinding at his ankle.

They hung poised in the tree, the two of them staring into each other's faces. For a moment, a shadow fell across her face, blotting it out, and then was gone. James felt goose bumps swarm over his back and down his arms. He looked away and then back, her enormous rage confronting him.

"Lemmie get down," James cried.

He turned and lowered himself from the tree, his mother backing her way down before him. James felt her grip along his back, and firmly on his upper arm as his feet touched the ground. He looked at the side of her face. He felt dangerously foolish. Violent emotions stirred in him. Already he was in deep trouble resulting from this minuscule and agonizingly short-lived rebellion.

I didn't do enough, he thought bitterly. He pulled wildly on his arm, hating the feel of her hand. Her grip tightened. She walked him briskly toward the house. The door to the house closed and the yard was silent. The vast old sycamore tree moved drowsily as a faint breeze stirred its limbs, a single board now spanning two lower branches.

James sat before his mother and father at the kitchen table. The table was lit by a cheap stained glass replica fixture hanging above. Matching Tupperware salt and pepper shakers sat next to a plastic napkin holder. It was Tuesday evening, which meant minute steak and green beans. The beans had pieces of bacon in them, limp and pale from being boiled.

"I've told you about that old tree," his mother said, smiling levelly. James wondered for the thousandth time what it would be like if he had brothers or sisters at the table with him.

"You never let me do anything," he said. Then more loudly, "My friends won't come here."

"James…," his father said. A threat hung in the air. The man's expression was sour, the corners of his mouth pulling down just a touch. *Who is he more irritated with?* James thought, *Her or me?* The older man's expression twitched.

James looked down at his food. The plastic dinner plate had a single paper napkin folded to the left of it. James never used napkins, yet there it sat at every meal. Cleaning up after dinner each night, James gingerly cleared away the used napkin next to his father's plate. Folded the same way. Wet in the same place.

James turned to his father, imploring.

"That's all she ever says. It's not safe," he said.

"Jimmy," his mother said in a level voice. "You give this up or you get up right now and go without your dinner."

James looked at his mother and then spoke to his father. "Ask her why the tree's not safe… ," he said.

"All right, go upstairs," his mother said, her voice rising. She leaned over to place a hand on the back of his chair, ready to pull it away as he stood. James stared at his father as he rose, tears welling up in his eyes. The tears of frustration disgusted him. He angrily wiped them away.

"Ask her!" James cried out. James' father looked away, as if from a doctor in the moment the needle penetrates his arm, closing himself off from the words. James glared at his mother, growing frantic. She calmly returned his gaze.

"Go to your room," she said flatly.

"Please, Momma," James whispered.

"God dammit, Jimmy!" his father barked, turning back, half rising from his chair. James stared directly at his mother as he rose from the table.

"I wish you were dead," he said.

James had been punished for his outburst. His father
had paddled him, using the wooden sorority paddle kept for
just that purpose. It had the name of his mother's college on
it. As always, James had to bend over and hold his ankles.
He had gone to his bed utterly humiliated, regretting the
pathetic apologies that tumbled out as the painful blows fell.

At 3 AM that night, his mother passed away.

His father had slept on, aware only later that his wife
had grown cold and still in the bed next to him. James,
asleep in his room, dreamt of a kettle squealing on a stove.
He awoke to hear his father rushing through the house;
yelling into the phone in the predawn darkness, and then
returning to their bed to flail about over the cold form of his
wife. It was later that a doctor told them a brain embolism
had killed her. A vein in her head had burst, flooding fragile
sections of her frontal lobe with reckless blood.

A few days later, her husband and her son stood side
by side as her hulking dark coffin was lowered into the
ground. James Hatch Sr. was stoic. James Hatch Jr. was
pale. The boy's eyes had a dull glazed quality. The boy
stood as the coffin disappeared into the dark earth,
exhausted and shivering in the July heat.

James sat upright in the middle of his bed, keeping his
feet tucked safely underneath him, his toes, and fingers far
back from the edge. He was wide-awake; trembling;
listening intently for any sound in the pitch-blackness. It
was the kind of absolute darkness that caused tiny firefly
sparks to wander along the edges of the boy's vision.

The clock in the living room chimed twice, distant and

faint and fell silent. The more he concentrated on the door he knew to be across from him, the more the darkness deepened. A single patch of moonlight, no more than a foot square, lay across the middle drawers of the dresser to his right. The watery blue light was slashed into thin strips by venetian blinds hanging at the head of the bed.

Time passed. He heard the distant water heater in the kitchen ignite. The burner flared for a few minutes and then fell quiet. A car passed on the street outside. The silence returned. Finally, James began to pray, clasping his hands and silently mouthing words. He felt a hard burning in his chest. Sweat ran down off his arms and face. He prayed fervently in the darkness, twisting his fingers into hard knots.

Eventually, the stream of words wound down to a halt. He drew his aching fingers apart and licked his dry lips. He pulled the sheets up closer around him. His neck and shoulders ached. His legs were numb. He became aware of how sweaty he was. The space beneath the sheets was like a furnace. The odor was acrid as he lifted them and let the stale air waft up past his face.

Maybe she's not coming, he thought.

He heard the sound, only barely audible, from across the room. A familiar prickling swarmed across his arms and neck. There was the faint click of the bedroom doorknob, once turned, being released. For a frantic moment, he thought of lurching off the bed toward the lamp on his dresser, then, an old reflex took over. He lay back on the bed, dragging the sheet across his exposed arms, and pretended to be asleep.

He heard another click as his bedroom door was gently pushed closed. A coolness swept across the room. He felt the sweat on his face chill. He remained motionless, splayed out at an odd angle on the bed, trying to breathe normally.

His eyelids began ticking convulsively.

The door to his closet opened. He heard a scraping sound as hangers were moved listlessly along the wooden dowel. He heard a faint scuffing as shoes were straightened on the floor. The door closed. There was a silence. Then the drawers of his dresser slid gently open one by one; the middle drawer groaning plaintively.

He was facing the dresser. Even under the covers, he could feel a bitter chill spreading across the front of his body. The sounds at his dresser ceased. There was a prolonged silence. He eased his eyes open to tiny slits. Before him were the familiar bands of moonlight but closer now by three feet. The bars of light illuminated the front of a woman's dress. One hand was visible, cold white in the moonlight, rhythmically clenching and unclenching. The other, partially in shadow, held a long straight kitchen knife. He closed his eyes again. The hairs on his neck crawled like a hive of bees. A voice whispered urgently, fading in and out like a weak radio signal. A twitch under his eye became more and more pronounced.

"...not safe," the voice hissed. "....not safe..."

Large trembling teardrops ran across his nose and down a cheek toward his ear. The tick in his face spread to his arm and down the right side of his body. The boy began to convulse.

Chapter 2: The Roof Fell In

James sat on the front step of the house; his bag packed beside him. Next to the small cement porch, was a dying cedar bush. Its limbs had been pared back over the years until it looked like a parody of a Japanese bonsai. Beyond it, toward the center of the yard, a newly planted maple stood, wired down with stakes to keep it upright in the steamy Texas sunshine. Otherwise, the lawn drifted in an unbroken green expanse down to the sidewalk.

Across the street, a man washed a long white Chevrolet. He looked up for a moment at James, and, shaking his head, returned to his work.

James rose to go in the house. He checked himself and sat down again. His stomach was full of butterflies. He took a deep breath. He had been invited to go to the Wilson Ranch for the weekend. Mr. Wilson, his son Warren, and other boys from the neighborhood were arriving any minute. Despite previous invitations, his mother had always refused to let him go. Now she could no longer stop him.

James recalled the morning of the first invitation, years ago, when he stood in the kitchen pleading with his mother. She dialed the phone, one arm clasping her robe shut as James stared at her dumbfounded; camping gear scattered about him on the kitchen floor.

"Hello, Mr. Wilson," she said. "Yes, this is James'

mother. Fine, thank you." She chewed her lip as the pleasantries continued.

"Mr. Wilson," she said. "I am sorry to call this close to your leaving for the ranch, but James can't go with you this time."

James was horrified. "Momma?" he moaned.

She waved him back with a hand.

"No, Mr. Wilson, he's not ill, I've just decided that a trip to the ranch wouldn't be a good idea at this time. No, he's fine."

James glanced about for his father, turning in abrupt panicked circles on the linoleum. "Mamma!" he said again, louder.

"Thank you for the offer. Perhaps another time," she concluded. "Thank you, good-bye." She hung up the phone and brushed a strand of hair out of her face. She pulled the robe tighter about her and turned to face him. Her features were drawn and pale.

James stared at her. Tears filled his eyes and ran down his face.

"Why did you do that?" he wailed.

"Because I have decided that it's not safe," she replied and turned to walk back to her bedroom. James started after her.

"Momma, what did I do wrong?" he said.

She turned. For a moment she looked at him. "You can't ever go to the Wilson ranch, Jimmy. It's not safe for you," she said. She turned and walked toward her bedroom, pausing at the door. She turned and looked at him, her features hardening.

"You think I like the way things are?" She clicked her tongue, as if preparing to speak more and then thought better of it. She turned, entered the bedroom, and closed the door softly behind her. James was left in the empty kitchen, surrounded by his bags.

"Jimmy?" The screen door opened behind him. He turned half around and looked up at his father. "You got everything?"

James flinched. He was unaccustomed to his father speaking to him. "I do."

"Alright, you stand up to your cousin Kevin. And mind everything Mr. Wilson tells you. You understand? I don't want to hear back."

"I understand," James said. "I'll mind. I will."

He looked up at his father. The silence between them was heavy and languid. His father rubbed his chin, looking out at the yard.

Mercifully, Mr. Wilson's big black Buick pulled up in front of the house. James took his bag and stepped off the porch. The car glided to the curb and the engine turned off. Mr. Wilson was the first out, followed by his son Warren. James' cousin Kevin followed them. Two more boys appeared. They stood by the car looking up toward the house. Kevin was big and broad shouldered for a fourteen-year-old. He was a head above any of the other boys, the shadow of a beard already on his chin. Mr. Wilson, immaculate in his workday lawyer's suit, walked across the yard to the porch.

"Hello, Jim," Mr. Wilson said, taking Mr. Hatch's hand. He turned to James. "James," said Mr. Wilson.

"Hello, sir," James said, squinting up at him.

"Warren, help him put his stuff in the trunk, will you? I'll be right there," Mr. Wilson said.

Mr. Wilson handed Warren the keys and turned back to talk to James' father, blocking him from view. They spoke in low voices. Mr. Wilson shook his head a little as he talked. James paused for a moment looking back. Then he turned and followed Warren to the car.

Warren opened the trunk and taking James' bag wedged it into an open spot beside the wheel well. James saw several rifle cases lying across the top of the bags and suitcases. To the left was a paper bag. Sticking out of the top, James saw the unmistakable multicolored wrapping paper of bottle rockets. There were two gross or more in the bag. James quickly did the math in his head. It was nearly 300 bottle rockets, maybe more. The Wilson's had money and Warren often had luxuries beyond those of any other of the boys. Being able to host guests at the ranch was just one of them. James looked up to realize Kevin and Warren were examining him closely. His frown grew as he looked back at them.

"What are you staring at," James said.

"You," Kevin said as he closed the trunk. "Just staring at you."

As darkness fell, Mr. Wilson drove on at a steady 75 miles per hour. Big trucks barreled up the highway behind them shifting left to the passing lane and roaring by, flooding the interior of the Buick with light and then plunging it into darkness. After a time, they were all quiet. The car passed through Columbus and leaving I-10, turned onto highway 90. The road went to two lanes and traffic became much lighter, trickling off into nothing by the time they passed through the next town.

Four boys were wedged in the back seat. James was against one door. Mike, the smallest of them, sat next to James, his head back against the seat, his mouth hanging open, wheezing. Kevin dozed against the far door. Sam had a pillow against Kevin's shoulder. James examined the three sleeping boys as the headlights from approaching cars threw racing patches of light across their faces. By 10 p.m., the Buick ran almost alone through the dark Texas landscape. James eventually drifted off, listening to the sound of the wind buffeting the car.

It was Easter. James, just three years old, had awoken before dawn to the sound of distant laughter from somewhere outside. He slid out of his small bed, gingerly making his way past toys scattered on his bedroom floor. His hand me down pajamas engulfed him. He crept along the hall and through the kitchen. Standing on tiptoes, he struggled to reach the handle of the back door. He opened and looked out into the darkness of the yard. Somewhere in the distance, the laughter sounded again. It was a child's laughter, bright and bubbly. He carefully opened the door and went out, closing the squeaky aluminum screen door gently behind. He stood barefoot, the cement of the back porch warm and damp under his feet. It was just before daybreak, the sun, a faint glimmer, plucking at the gray darkness in the east.

Porch lights burned from neighbor's houses, partially visible through the patchwork of leaves that bounded the back of the yard. The grass, freshly mown, smelled sweetly.

James heard the laughter again, more clearly. It came from the old sycamore tree in the back of the yard. The huge tree was bounded one side by a rusting rose trellis, now in ruins, the plants long dead. The trellis itself dated from before the war. Made of metal piping and spanned by heavy cattle wire. It was a reminder of the two old sisters his parents had bought the house from before he was born. Most of their decorative touches had since been torn up and hauled away. Only the trellis remained to be demolished.

James stood staring out into the dimness. There was a patch of paleness, a blur among the branches of the sycamore. It was a light spot against the darkness of the void. Again he heard the laughter. He looked up at the sky overhead, awash with stars, the brightest of which flashed green, gold, red and blue. The moon was a tiny sliver, barely visible, leaving the stars to run riot in the night sky.

James crossed the yard toward the old tree, his tiny steps carrying him across the endless expanse of grass. The recently mown grass was prickly under his feet. When he reached the trellis, the tree rose above him.

There in the branches something was moving slowly down toward him.

"Jimmy!" his mother's called from the house. The porch light came on. She stepped onto the porch and called again. "Jimmy!"

He turned and ran giggling up to the house, his little figure tottering side to side as he emerged from the darkness.

"Why are you out here again?" she said, half to herself. She took the toddler in her arms and hugged him close. "C'mon now, we're gonna be late for Sunrise service."

She took the boy inside and closed the door.

The car drove into Luling with the boys still dozing. They passed a darkened boarded-up movie house.

"Sorry," Warren would later explain. "The roof fell in." and leave it at that, like they should just understand that the roof fell in and nobody was going to fix it.

They rolled past dark and silent churches. On Sunday morning, Mr. Wilson would be going into to town to attend church and then returning home to take the boys to lunch at the local cafe. James woke to the sound of gravel grinding underneath the wheels. The boys stirred. Mr. Wilson pulled the car into the parking lot of a late-night grocery. They piled out.

A big glowing orange sign on the roof of the store said Pick-N-Pak #3. Light flooded out of the plate glass windows on the front of the store. The smallest boy, Mike, spit on the smooth green pavement. It was his nervous habit to spit constantly. The boys filed into the store. A single spindly comic book rack stood by the door, displaying dog-eared, out of date comics. The aisles held racks of candy bars and canned food. The floor was old red and white squares of linoleum worn thin and pale in front of the register. Slim-Jims and fuzzy key chains hung on a display atop the counter. Cigarettes, batteries, and extension cords covered the wall behind. An old woman stood expressionless by the register, a cigarette between her nicotine-stained fingers.

Without any direction from Mr. Wilson, the other boys began collecting various groceries. James took a candy bar and walking to the counter, laid a wrinkled dollar down next to it. Mr. Wilson, who was looking out at the highway, heard James, and turned.

"Your daddy gave me enough money for you." He handed James back his dollar. "You keep this for later." James looked up into Mr. Wilson's face. He saw little there to clarify what the man was meaning for him to do. He took the dollar back, embarrassed.

James turned to see Warren and Kevin arriving at the counter with breakfast cereal, bread, lunch meat, and potato chips. Mike walked up with two boxes of chocolate snack cakes. He stopped for a moment and looked at James. "You better get some food," he said.

With a start, James headed down the aisle following Sam. He stopped next to him and held up a can of soup. "Like this?" he asked.

Sam shook his head. "No, no, man. Spaghetti O's, Fig

Newtons, Oreos, you know? Get what you want." he finished emphatically.

James replaced the can of soup and picked up two more cans of spaghetti. They split and James headed on towards the back of the store. He grabbed a loaf of bread, peanut butter, and a jar of jelly. He passed brightly lit glass coolers. He stopped for a half gallon of milk and then, pausing to look up toward Mr. Wilson, took chocolate milk instead. He closed the door and headed back to the front of the store. He passed an alcove leading to the rest rooms and stopped. Something shifted in the shadows. It shambled forward, rotten and bloated. The stink of decay rolled out into the store. A pink tongue licked out.

The glass jar of jelly hit the floor and burst. James backed into the display counter, dropping more items. Cans of food crashed to the floor. To get his balance, James raked his arm back along the top shelf sending a dozen bags of chips tumbling off. The thing in the shadows, shambling on four legs, rubbed itself along the wall, coming almost into the light. A piece of rotting meat hit the floor with a loud wet slap.

"Jimmy!" a voice, said.

James looked up into Mr. Wilson's face.

"Are you all right?" Mr. Wilson said taking his arm, steadying him.

James looked at Mr. Wilson and back to the alcove. It was empty.

"Are you all right, Jimmy?" Mr. Wilson repeated.

"I'm okay," James said. He continued to look back over his shoulder at the alcove as Mr. Wilson led him on toward the front counter. James saw the boys clustered at the end of the aisle staring at him.

"…really is nuts," Sam said under his breath.

"You boys pick those things up. I'm taking Jimmy out

to the car," Mr. Wilson said as he walked James unceremoniously past the counter and out through the glass doors. He took James out and sat him down in the back seat of the car. Mr. Wilson stood with the door swung open. The old woman from the store came out to the car.

"Is he all right?" she asked. She turned to Mr. Wilson. "You don't want me to call anybody?"

"No, he'll be fine," said Mr. Wilson. She walked back toward the store. She stopped at the front of the car and looked back again. Shadows writhed about her. Small twisters of darkness spun under the glow of the florescent lights. Mr. Wilson looked at James for a moment and then he spoke.

"Jimmy, are you feeling all right?"

James blinked at the bright windows of the store.

"Are you sick?"

James continued to stare ahead. After a pause, Mr. Wilson bent down to look in at James. "You're not high on anything are you, son?" he said quietly.

James looked up, startled, "No way, No sir."

"Well, alright," Mr. Wilson said, apparently satisfied with the boy's emphatic response. "You stay here." He looked at James a moment longer, drew a deep breath, and turned to head back to the store. James sat, shaken and sick to his stomach in the big car. He listened intently for any sound above the whine of tires along the highway. He waited, sweaty and short of breath, until the boys all filed out the door toward the car.

James was dressed in his best Sunday clothes. He was four years old. He went with his mother and father to St. Andrews Presbyterian Church on a bright Saturday in September. A cool breeze rippled the taller grass along the church hedge. The air was chilly. As he tottered along, he and his parents joined the hushed crowd filing into the church.

A woman at the organ played muted music. Seated on the polished wooden pew near the front of the church, James stared up at the stained-glass windows along the sanctuary hall. There was a white bird depicted slashing open its own chest, its young lapping at the red flowing blood. Another window depicted Christ walking on the Sea of Galilee, stormy waves washing about his feet. He studied the big unadorned wooden cross hanging at the front. He was bored.

The service began. Everyone in the church stood for a hymn. James obediently slid off the seat cushion and stood on the floor, lost between the high-backed pews. After a time, the singing ceased. He was lifted back to his seat. His mother placed one arm about him. He began to squirm. She took hold of his arm and leaned down over him. Her grip was firm.

"Shush," she said. He sat for a few minutes before boredom again became too much and he began to squirm. His mother lifted him to her lap and placed her arms about him. James could see over the top of the pews. He stopped squirming and sat still in the warmth of his mother's arms. She rocked him gently humming softly in his ear.

James saw the hats of ladies and the necks of men, their stiff white collars extending above the dark fabric of their suits. Three red-carpeted steps led up to a long dark box. Flowers surrounded it. James looked down the pew to his left and saw a dark-haired man. Next to him was a boy his age, his cousin, Kevin. As James watched, his cousin stared ahead unseeing. James' brow furrowed as he looked back at the coffin. He watched the minister. The man's voice was flat and listless. It droned on gently.

James felt his mother turn. Her body became rigid and

tense beneath him. He felt her take a breath and hold it. He followed her gaze down the pew to the right and saw a woman standing in the aisle, just to the left of a broad brick pillar. She was the only person, save the minister, standing in the church. Her light-colored dress was stained red across the lower half.

"Aunt Margie," James said loudly. He smiled broadly. "Aunt Margie," he turned and repeated. He looked up into the eyes of his mother. She was now staring at him; her head still half turned toward the bloody figure in the aisle. Her mouth hung slightly open, and as she breathed out across the side of his face, her breath became sour, smelling of bile. The color drained from her skin.

The woman by the pillar turned toward them, her expression vaguely confused, red ran down the side of her head.

James looked around at Kevin. He extended his small arm and pointed. "Aunt Margie," he said smiling at the stricken boy. His small high voice echoed in the church. The minister had stopped speaking. Kevin's eyes traced the line of sight still indicated by James' tiny finger pointing toward the empty alcove at the end of the pew. Kevin frantically searched the alcove with his eyes. He began kicking and screaming.

James' mother was rigid beneath him. She placed her white-gloved hand over the boy's hand and slowly lowered it. She pushed him from her lap onto the cushion.

Only once did he attempt to move again during the funeral. His fear of his mother's apparent anger easing a little, he rose to look around. She took his arm and ground the small bones side to side beneath her hand. When the memorial ended, they took him and left the church. When they arrived home, his mother hauled him, half-dangling off the floor, to his room.

She sat him crying loudly on the bed, towering over him.

"What did you see?" Her face was red with rage.

"Aunt Margie," James said, tears streaming down his face. He began to bawl louder.

"What did you see?" she repeated.

"Aunt Margie!" he wailed, snot running down his lip.

"You did not see Aunt Margie!" his mother hissed in reply, yanking him roughly up to his feet.

"Aunt Margie!" he screamed back terrified.

"You didn't see her. You did not see your Aunt Margie! You're lying to me!" She grabbed a wire hanger and whipped him half a dozen times to drive the point home.

"Jimmy, I hope you like saltine crackers cuz that's all we got for you," Mike said. He spit on the ground. James sat up in the car seat. Kevin dropped a bag of groceries on his lap.

"Nothing breakable," Kevin said, as he got in.

The doors slammed shut and Mr. Wilson started the car.

"That old woman is gonna be mopping up all night," Warren said over the seat at James. Mr. Wilson, who had been backing out, put the car in park. He turned and looked at Warren.

"That's enough," he said.

Warren quickly turned around and sat still.

Mr. Wilson put the car into drive. They rolled out of the parking lot and back onto the highway. James sat in the darkness of the back seat. They all remained quiet as Mr. Wilson drove out of Luling toward the ranch house a few miles beyond the town limits.

James turned his face to the window. "Sorry, " he said

weakly to no one in particular. Warren faced steadily forward in the front seat, saying nothing.

"What's up with you, Jimmy?" Kevin asked him. The tone of Kevin's voice was neutral. He was turned toward James in the shadows.

"That'll be enough, Kevin," Mr. Wilson said in a low voice.

James looked at dark fields as they swept by. The stars hung high in the sky, glowing fiercely. A full moon had risen about the trees, throwing pale light across the open spaces. Mesquite trees and bull nettle crowded the fence lines along the road. Dried grass stood stark and stiff, thrashing wildly in the red glow of the taillights as the car raced by.

Shortly, Mr. Wilson pulled off the highway. A driveway led up to a single-story white stone ranch house with a long flat cement porch. He got out, unlocked the front door of the house, and walked in, switching on lights. A big green and brown spider clung to a web spanning two of the wrought iron pillars supporting the front porch. The intricate web was the size of a garbage can lid. It quivered in the summer air as the screen door slammed.

The boys ate their fill and retired to Warren's bedroom. By eleven, the lights were out. James lay in his bedroll on a green army camp cot. He listened to the boys talk in the cool darkness, saying nothing. Their voices grew drowsier. Finally, the room fell silent save for the drone of the air conditioner.

Chapter 3: McCollough

James dreamt of a storm, of trees bent double under the onslaught of a raging wind, and of lightning so close that the hot sharp smell of ozone beat against his face. He stood in the darkened parlor of an unfamiliar house that groaned and strained under the brutal lashing of wind and rain. Lightning lit the inside in raw white stripes. Thunder shook the walls, dropping framed and aging photos to the floor. Standing at a window, James looked out.

In the darkness, he made out the shape of a low cistern, a windmill squealing wildly above it in the storm. A blast of lightning laid a blinding white light across the yard. It turned the torrential rain into bright gauze obscuring the open ground. James saw a gigantic oak tree towering over the well. Two figures could just be made out on either side of the cistern. Then darkness fell again, blotting out the yard.

James placed his face against the window. The glass was brutally cold.

Being so close to the glass is a bad idea, he thought to himself as he continued to stare into the storming darkness. A blast of thunder rolled across the house. Somewhere in a distant room, he heard glass shatter.

Again the lightning flashed. Through the rain-blurred glass, James could see a figure had moved toward him.

Again, darkness blotted out the yard.

"Get back from the window," he heard a woman's flat dead voice say from somewhere in the room behind him. He turned and looked at the bare room. "Momma?" he said. He slowly turned back, wiping the glass before him, and stared, expectation rising in him.

The seconds ticked by. Rain lashed at the window. James saw a vague white blur just beyond the glass, there in the darkness. A blast of lightning brought a woman's face he did not recognize into stark illumination not six inches beyond the pane of glass. Below her chin, a red blur of gore ran down her chest.

James awoke with a start in the darkness of the bedroom. For the briefest moment he thought he was home. Then his hand touched the edge of the camp cot and he remembered where he was.

He lay back for a moment, letting panic recede and listening to the drone of the air conditioner. The air was startlingly cold. It smelled of freshly laundered cotton sheets and gun oil. In the darkness around him, James could sense the closeness of the other boys sleeping, their gentle breathing drowned out by the air conditioner.

He rose from his sleeping bag and stood rubbing his arms in the chill air. Taking a tentative step toward the door, James felt his toes brush the stiff metal leg of a bed. He curled them under protectively and, running his fingertips along the edge of the mattress made his way to the door. He touched an unknown arm and quickly withdrew his hand. He found the door handle and turning it, stepped into the hall.

The floor was chalky and dry underneath his bare feet. He pulled the bedroom door to. The sound of the air conditioner became distant and muffled, the air was now much warmer. James could hear the rhythmic chirp of a cricket somewhere in the house. He relieved himself in the small bathroom off the kitchen and entered the darkened den. He went to the large plate glass window that looked out onto the driveway. It was bathed in the bright light of the single bulb mounted outside above the window. A pool of light fell across James' legs and onto the floor at his feet.

Big fluttering moths circled frantically beyond the glass, creating an island of bright motion in the stillness. They collided, throwing themselves against the bright hot bulb. Beyond them, blooms of azalea bushes stood motionless against the white fence bordering the driveway. The warm air in the den raised a moist sheen on James' skin, sending a wave of goose bumps across his arms and legs.

Before him, the empty strip of Highway 90 shimmered. Brightly lit signs illuminated a distant highway intersection far to the right. A car swung into view, its headlights throwing dappled patterns against the fence and the front of the house. It raced by, receding into the darkness, two tiny red dots. James felt a deep shuddering breath fill his chest. He watched the taillights until they winked out. The road was a dark ribbon of stillness.

Then he saw a flash of emerald on the pavement of the driveway. A cicada lay on its back, fanning its wings in a futile effort to fly. James unlocked the door and stepped barefoot outside. He was careful not to slam the screen door. The drone of crickets rose and fell from across the fields. He took a few steps and bent down over the big green insect. James picked it up between his index finger and thumb. Two hard black eyes regarded James for a moment, then the wings beat a frenzy of motion, raising a harsh buzz. The insect, seeking the open sky, had flown down against the brightly lit pavement, grinding against the rough surface.

"Wait a minute, now," James said.

The struggling legs felt like a small wire brush. James held it out before him, its wide head facing in toward the curve of his thumb. Free, the wings beat frantically, whirring against his open fingers. He held it near to his face, like a tiny buzzing fan. The cicada's body was a deep shining green. Its wings were shot through with rainbows of color. The insect would exhaust itself against the cement and by morning it would be stripped by red ants.

James tossed the cicada up into the night air. It banked above the driveway and disappearing for a moment above the roofline, returned to thump itself against the hard pavement.

"Oh, c'mon," James said.

He captured the insect again, and cupping it in his hands, stepped into the damp grass beside the driveway. He rounded the corner of the house entering deep shadow. In the back of the yard, a bright utility light was mounted atop a pole. James threw the cicada up again. He heard it whir off into the darkness, headed for the distant light. At the last moment, James saw its tiny form bank and disappear into the dark bulk of an oak tree.

It was then that James saw a figure standing in the shadows beneath the tree, stock still, facing him. The boy backed up against the house, straining to hear anything above the distant hum of the air conditioner around the far side. The figure stepped into the light. It was an old man, bent and haggard. James shook his head. A strange buzzing filled his ears, a keening, buzzing sound. The old man laughed at him.

James became aware that ants were swarming his foot, stinging. He brushed them away and took another step back, preparing to turn and run for the front.

The old man came forward, swaying under a wide brimmed hat that shaded his face from the bright tungsten light above him. In the hat's shadow, his face was a pale chalky blur, his eyes two dark stains on the shifting whiteness. Behind him, out of the blackness, a dog appeared, moving slowly, head down, nose to the ground. Two more dogs followed, circling in from beneath the oak. James became aware of more dogs, now half a dozen, now a dozen, rising from the shadows around the old man.

James took another step back, one knee trembling uncontrollably.

"I know all about you, boy. Stirring em all up, you are. Waking *him* up," the old man said, his voice shattering the stillness. "Listen," he said. "You got the ear for it, listen. They're all talkin' about you."

James heard a drone of whispers rising in his ears.

"Get over here, boy, before you do something none of us can undo," the old man said, shuffling forward.

James turned and dashed around the corner into the glare of the driveway. He yanked the screen door open, fumbling with the front door handle and burst through into the house, quickly closing the door behind him. He stood panting and shuddering in the silence, his back against the door. He groped for the dead bolt. His fingers found it and he turned the knob, feeling the bolt slide into place. To his left, a broad pool of yellow light fell on the floor from the large picture window. He leaned against the door, listening, his ears straining for the sound of movement on the driveway.

A ragged shadow crossed the pool of light. For a moment, it paused. James felt lightheaded. He pressed himself flat, looking across his shoulder toward the window. From this angle, he was able to make out a single gnarled hand visible against the glass. The shadow crossed on, coming towards him. The screen door swung open, and James heard a hand settle against the doorknob. He held his breath.

A voice whispered. "Get out here, boy. Now."

The door handle rattled violently for a moment.

"Come out wherever you are..." The old man's voice was a low raspy sing song.

Too afraid to move, James eyed the doorway to the kitchen, indistinct in the dimness. The mail slot creaked open directly between his legs. A small pool of light shone on the floor by his feet.

"You stand out like a road flare boy," the old man said, speaking low, his voice emerging down by the mail slot. James could see long dirty fingers tracing the edges. One finger brushed the fabric of his pajama legs.

"You and me? We're a rare kind," the old man continued. "We got the gift, that's what it is. It's bad enough for a woman to have the gift, but a man? A man gets the sight once every hundred years. It's always a dark thing... And here we are two of us. How dark will it get, I wonder?" There was a long pause. "You brought your mother here?" he said, surprise creeping into his voice.

James felt a shock. An image of his mother thrust itself into his head. She stood in the still moonlight next to a big cement water cistern. A windmill turned slowly above her. James tried to draw a breath. It came no further than the back of his tongue, tasting bitter.

"Smart one she is. She's got a taste for the water at the well," the old man said. The aging fingers wriggled vigorously along the edges of the mail slot, making a dry raspy sound. James' eye was twitching badly.

"Ever seen a hawk take a mouse, boy? That mouse don't even have time to blink," the old man said his voice rising. Somewhere off in the distance a dog howled in pain.

"She told you not to come here, but you just wouldn't listen, would you?" The mail-slot clanged shut.

"Jimmy saw McCollough by the house last night," Warren said eating his cereal. Milk ran down his chin as he pried the spoon out of his mouth sideways. Sunlight shone into the kitchen through a wide window over the sink. Mr. Wilson stood by the counter. He wore dark round-toed work boots; scarred by cactus and barbed wire. He picked up his work gloves and his yellow straw Stetson.

"You saw Mr. McCollough here?" Mr. Wilson asked James. James nodded yes.

"He described him to a tee. Dogs, too," Warren said.

"Well, he's a long way from home. At least for him," Mr. Wilson said. He picked up a battered gallon jug of drinking water from the counter. "I'll check on him. After that, I'll be over at the new feed barn." he said. "Also, Mr. Hagel is storing some equipment in the old barn till it sells. So, for the time being, it'll be locked."

"I understand," Warren replied. Mr. Wilson walked through the den and out the back door. The screen door slammed behind him. The boys heard the truck start up. It drove past the house and out onto the highway.

"That McCollough is nuts," James ventured.

Kevin bent down to tie his shoe. "You're one to talk," he said.

The boys rose, put their dishes in the sink and walked into the bedroom. They unzipped the rifle bags. In a few minutes there were two shotguns, two rifles, and a short barreled .38 revolver lying on the bed. James gawked at the guns. Except for single shot .22 rifles at scout camp, he had never been around guns. The most impressive was a Remington .20-gauge semi-automatic shotgun. The barrel was long and blue with a ventilated rib running down the top to the ball sight on the end.

"Good way to go through a whole box of shells," was all Warren had to say about it.

There was also a semi-automatic Ruger .22 rifle with a scope. It had two little clips of ammunition next to it. Warren lifted the .22 rifle, made sure the chamber was cleared, and sprayed it methodically inside and out with a blue can of WD-40 lubricant. He laid it down and then did the same with the shotguns, the other rifle and finally the pistol. He put the pistol into a holster on his belt and took the .22 rifle with the scope.

The boys deferred to Kevin to pick next. He picked up the Remington and opened the box of 20-gauge shells. He stuffed a dozen in his two front pockets. Next in the order, an order they all knew and understood, was Sam who selected the single shot .410 shotgun. Mike took the last rifle, a scuffed up .22 single shot. James went empty handed.

Warren put on a battered Australian bush hat with one side of the brim buttoned up. He pushed his black hair out of the way and pulled the chinstrap down. He sprayed his bare arms with insect repellent and handed it off. James felt a strange exultation to be part of this silent preparation. It was his only experience of being an insider, however tenuous. The boys made a last check of their supplies and then filed out the back door into the warm morning air.

The boys crossed the highway, stepped through a barbed wire fence, climbed a sloping hillside, and struck off along a cow path that led along the side of the hill and on toward the pastures beyond. On the high ground to their right, they passed an old two-story barn surrounded by smaller sheds, fencing, and gates.

They walked single file down a narrow cow path.

Already the heat of the day was rising. After a while, the boys came upon a big rusting square of corrugated tin lying flat just off the path.

Warren bent down and took the corner of the tin sheet in his hand. Kevin stood next to him and held the shotgun, its barrel pointed down. Warren lifted the tin sheet and in one motion, raised it upright and stepped back. Beneath it, the ground was dark with moisture. A large centipede unwound itself and scurried away. Bugs swarmed through a tangle of pale roots which lay flattened against the dirt. A single tan and sinuous body broke into motion covering ground away from the boys with startling speed. The shotgun kicked and the concussion boomed off toward the distant overpass and then echoed back. The sharp smell of gunpowder filled the morning air. The snake flopped and wriggled; its mid-section parted neatly in two next to a smoking hole in the moist earth. The meat of its body was pink and bright. Its movements slowed and stopped.

James stared at the dead snake. His ears rang from the gunshot, the tone rising higher and higher. Kevin prodded the snake with the tip of his shoe.

"Copperhead," he said.

"You totally wasted him," Mike said. Each time he blurted out something, his eyes darted from face to face. The other boys offered him little back. He spit on the snake.

The snake's head, shaped like a triangle, had eyes slit top to bottom like a cat. Its body was the softest and most sinuous combination of tan and brown. A glittering sheen ran along its perfect scales down to the ugly wound. Blood pooled in the dirt. Red ants began to run about frantically over the exposed pink flesh. Warren dropped the piece of tin siding back in place, blotting out the sight of it.

Early one spring morning, James, just four years old,

stood by the old air conditioning cooling tower that leaned drunkenly in the back yard of his family's house. The cooling tower had once rained down a glittering cascade of water, used by the 1950's era air conditioning system to cool the house. Now it was a teetering wreck, its horizontal planks of wood warped and burnt gray by the sun. On the ground around the base of the cooling tower, a pool of water still collected from a single, slowly dripping spigot. The ground was soft and moist, the grass tall and green next to the base of the tower where the lawn mower couldn't reach. Behind those slim emerald leaves of grass, beneath the tower, was a dark secret space hidden from view.

Placing the bulk of the tower between himself and the house where his mother was washing the morning dishes, the boy dropped down on his small knees and parted the foot high leaves of slender grass. Coolness rolled out across his arms. Within the opening, he saw tiny distinct motions. Pill bugs wheeled about and headed away from the light. A June bug fell clumsily from its perch and climbed again, rising along the leaves of grass, it's bulky body jiggling with awkward effort.

James' small hands reached in, his eyes glowing brightly. Behind the wall of dark green grass, blocked from the sun, the grass was pale yellow. The ground was musty; hidden in damp shadow. James touched the soft ground. He drew his fingers back, muddy with rot and the sickly-sweet smell of decay. He shifted his position and reached in further. He felt something take hold of his hand, as if someone had gripped him firmly with forefinger and thumb. He struggled to straighten up and withdraw his hand. The moments in which the length of his small arm passed from darkness into light seemed interminable, like reeling a fish up out of deep water.

He looked up to see his mother next to him. She wore

yellow rubber dishwashing gloves still wet with soapy water. She had kicked off her shoes. Her eyes were wide with panic. In her hand, was a long silver kitchen knife, its blade flashing brittle and cold. James looked back at his hand, now fully out in the light. Two eyes, slit top to bottom like a cat's, looked back. He drew his hand up higher. A shining body coiled out of the darkness, longer and unbelievably longer. He was puzzled and frightened. He started to turn, his eyes wide. He felt a wet glove crush his arm flat to the earth, driving his face into the hot green grass.

Unable to rise, the weight of her body across him, James heard the blade slashing repeatedly through the grass and mud just beyond the tips of his small pink fingers. He twisted hard to raise his head and look past the wall of dazzling green grass that blocked his view. Then he was yanked to his feet, muddy and dazed and carried towards the car. As he jolted along, he stared at the body of the serpent dangling from his mother's yellow-gloved hand.

Chapter 4: Stirring the Mud

"Jimmy!" James realized the boys were yelling his name. They stood up the path; hands on hips, staring back his way.

"What a stoner!" Mike called out. He was growing increasingly giddy about his newfound status. Among these neighborhood boys, he had always been the runt. But now, despite all his failings, was no longer the low boy on the pecking order. Each joke he made at James' expense, was a confirmation that he belonged, and James did not. His pleasure was palpable.

James shook his head and caught up to them. A new fence line closed in on the left as they walked. Thick brush and scrub rose on the right. They continued in single file with Warren in the lead.

"Put your safeties on," Warren said over his shoulder.

"Don't shoot your dick off," Mike tittered.

"For god's sake, please shut up," Sam said, cuffing Mike on the back of his head.

Cicadas droned in the morning heat. Locusts leapt up in their path, buzzing away. Mesquite limbs hung out into the trail. Wicked thorns two to three inches long stood out on the branches. There was bull nettle closer to the ground, and cactus, every plant crowding the hard packed stony cow path. They passed fire ant beds. Circular spaces, the size of garbage can lids, with nothing growing, just a circle of bleached stones with a small hole at the middle. Long lines of red ants raced along the trail. They moved with a frantic speed to finish their work before the ground became too hot.

The steep hillside was impenetrable, a tangle of trees and brush which had never been cleared. Only the more open level pastures were mowed. The boys passed onto a double rutted dirt road made over the years by ranch trucks passing through. In a thin strip down the middle of the road, stunted plants grew dwarfed, and exposed. The space became less crowded and close around them. Cresting another steep hill, the truck path dropped down. To their right, the foliage opened to reveal a small pond, no bigger than a backyard swimming pool. It was set down on a natural terrace cut into the side of the hill, its surface was choked with dark water plants, the muddy bank crisscrossed with deep hoof prints.

Warren raised his .22 and sighting through the scope fired two shots in quick succession. Mud splattered at the edge of the water. James heard two splashes as something entered the water at two spots along the bank. He looked back to where Warren's shots had struck. He made out the struggling form of a brown bullfrog in the mud. So close in color was it to the reddish clay at the pond's edge that it was nearly impossible to see at a distance. From where James stood, it looked as if some invisible hand was stirring a small patch of the mud. Taking big steps, Warren dashed through the cactus and bull nettle, down the slope of the hill toward the pond. Sam followed. They reached the bank and circled along it.

Warren raised the twitching form of a two-foot-long bullfrog. James had never seen animals being shot. First the snake and now this frog in its death throes. The shimmering brown body hung quivering in Warren's hand. A drop of red fell. It was a strangely detached feeling, watching the animal die, its death casually dismissed by the other boys.

Warren tossed the bullfrog unceremoniously into the pond. It hit the muddy water and disappeared. Warren and Sam climbed back up the side of the hill. When he reached the path again, Warren set the butt of the rifle on the ground. He took off his glasses and his hat. His hair was already soaked with sweat. He pulled it behind his ear and replaced the hat firmly on his head. He wiped his square gold rim glasses and put them on again. James watched Warren, feeling vaguely uncomfortable. The animal had continued to twitch after it had been shot. He was not entirely sure that it was not now drowning.

Kevin produced a cigarette and lit it. The sky was growing cloudy.

"Gimmie a hit," Sam said. Kevin handed it over in an easy practiced motion.

"Don't leave cigarette butts on my property," Warren said over his shoulder.

Kevin took the cigarette back and started down the path following Warren, a puff of blue smoke rising as he walked.

"You get first shot at everything, Warren," said Mike.

"That's cuz you're too slow," Warren replied, not bothering to turn around.

They walked for a while longer. Mike spit, to very little effect.

"Let me use your rifle, then I could hit something," said Mike.

"Maybe, later," said Warren.

Mike frowned. He rubbed his hand across his fuzzy head of hair and continued walking.

The boys stood by an open field that had been recently mowed. Foot-tall mesquites were already springing up. To the left, a barbed wire fence continued along. It disappeared into the trees near a big four-lane overpass. The whine of cars and the drone of big trucks were continual in the distance. Warren pointed to the trees that ran across on the far side of the field.

"That's Plum Creek," he said to James.

In the distance, a large flock of black grackles milled about squawking and feeding. Sam raised the .410 shotgun high and fired. The pellets rained down on the distant birds. They rose as one and circled off, to set down further away. Sam broke open the shotgun and removed the slender red plastic shotgun shell. Smoke drifted out of the ragged open end of it. James took the shell from him and admired it. It smelled of fireworks.

The boys walked through the open fields towards the huge highway overpass that crossed Plum Creek. Beneath it, trees obscured the green water of the creek moving slowly by. As they got closer, trucks and cars passing overhead beat out a dull staccato on the tons of cement that formed the highway above them. They entered the dense tree line. Here it was very different than the sun-blasted hill sides behind them. The trees watered by the creek were not stunted. They were full grown oaks and maples, growing in the bottom land along the creek's gently meandering course.

The creek itself was about fifteen feet wide at the water level, but deep, as much as ten feet in places, and lined by steeply angled banks. The large trees hung over the water creating a natural canopy. Massive trunks lay in the cool shadows, uprooted at flood stage, and carried there to form a resting place for turtles, red eared sliders whose green shells gleamed in the cool shade.

On the far bank, a log lay half out of the water. On its

upstream side was an ever-growing island of greenery and trash collecting in the slow current. Beer cans and bottles lay half in the water, buoyed by the floating debris.

Warren handed his rifle to Mike who, in turn, handed his single shot .22 to James. James turned the rifle over in his hands and opened the breech. A single copper-colored .22 shell flipped out and fell onto the bank. James picked up the shell. It was long and thin between his fingers, cool to the touch. He wiped the little bullet on his pants and reloaded the gun.

Warren took his pistol out of its holster and leveling it on the far bank, drew a breath and let it out. Mike scooted up the bank to put himself behind the tip of the pistol barrel. Warren fired. The underpass rang like a tin drum. A gray cloud of smoke rose through shafts of sunlight. Warren drew another breath and fired again. The neck of the bottle shattered. It dropped out of the tangled mass of floating branches and disappeared in a trail of bubbles.

Mike raised the rifle and peered through the scope. He set the cross hairs on one and squeezed. The can jumped six inches. He sank the can with another shot.

"How about that?" said Mike.

"It's thirty feet away," said Kevin.

"Suck my dick," said Mike.

James laughed out loud.

"What's so funny, Jimmy" Kevin said, looking past Mike. His face grew red.

James stopped smiling.

"I'm not taking any shit from you, Jimmy," Kevin said, not taking his eyes off James.

"Fine, whatever," James said, looking away.

"If you're gonna hang around, wipe that stupid grin off your face." Kevin finished. He turned and walked off along the bank of the creek.

Mike stared after Kevin for a moment.

"Better watch it, Jimmy," he said.

"I guess he doesn't like me!" James yelled at Kevin's receding back.

"So, don't laugh at him," Warren said, taking his rifle back from Mike.

The boys rose and prepared to follow Kevin. James didn't get up. Mike stopped and looked at him. He felt a twinge of sympathy mixed with guilt; a feeling entirely new for the smaller boy. It puzzled him. "If you're gonna sit here by yourself, you might as well shoot at cans." Mike said. He handed James a handful of .22 shells.

"You really staying here?" Warren asked, his exasperation showing.

"I'll catch up," James said.

Warren shrugged and walked away. "Don't aim up, .22 long rifle will travel a mile," he hollered back over his shoulder. James watched, as the boys trailed away down the creek, their conversation fading into the trees.

"Some family thing I guess," he heard Sam say.

James exhaled. Tension leaked out of him in a ragged rush of air. He listened to the soft slurring of water in the creek. Ripples spread. The dark green shadow of a fish appeared in the slow green current.

James was not at all surprised at how the group was behaving. Though he had known these boys in the neighborhood most of his life, the social isolation his mother enforced on him, for her impenetrable reasons, made him an outsider. He had spent his life being the target of other boys. Only Mr. Wilson's authority had allowed him to be on this trip. James knew it, and he was willing to pay the price just to be out in the world, free from his mother's endless fears. He turned the small rifle over in his hands. This world was *intoxicating*.

He cocked the little .22, raised it, and sighted down the scuffed blue barrel at a target. The tiny ball at the end of the barrel lining up in the "v" of the top sight was big enough to blot out most of the dirty coke can that lay against the far bank. He fired. Mud splattered next to the can. He lifted and pulled back the lever on the .22, and a spent brass casing flipped out, landing in the sandy dirt. James took a shell out of his pocket. He gingerly put the new shell in the breech and closed it. He cocked the gun by pulling straight back on the round knob at the back of the barrel and sighted again on the can.

His second shot stuck a clean hole in the can, turning it over against the bank. He set the rifle's scarred butt upright against the ground. He leaned on it and studied his shot. Something seemed out of place. He shielded his eyes from a bright spot on the water and looked closer. He saw vague shadows stirring along the shallows, moving up the bank. He felt pressure growing in his head, his hair standing up along the back of his neck.

"Oh, no," he whispered.

Along the far bank, a layer of grayness, like mist, rose out of the water and crept up toward the can. James leaned in, staring. Slowly, shapes began to form in the grayness, elongated sinuous shapes.

James gathered his feet under him. A gentle breeze set the leaves along the creek rippling. The shadows trembled and vanished. James looked up and down the creek. The water flowed peacefully along. A bright red cardinal flew across his line of vision and landed in a tree. James studied the bird. It leapt nimbly from limb to limb, alternately lost from sight and then visible again in the dark greenery. The sun was climbing overhead. A breeze came again, stirring the warm air.

In the next moment, James was completely

submerged. Water swirled about him in violent black torrents. A coughing cold swept up, seizing his arms and legs, tumbling him violently and then, instantly, the water was gone. He sat on the sandy bank of the creek. Sunshine played across the trunks of trees. The cardinal leapt to another branch and turning, flew off through the trees, dipping and rising in its flight. James' heart beat wildly in his chest. He shuddered, fingering his dry shirt, and staring about him.

A stirring of expectation filled him. *Something's coming,* he thought. Across the way, the leaves formed a dense wall of greenery. The breeze had died and did not return. James slowly rose, backing his way up the steepness of the bank. He spotted the rifle, below where he had left it. He forced his feet to step downward closer to the water. He bent slowly and took hold of the rifle. Something was brushing up against him. His scalp crawled as if covered with ants. He backed up the bank. Voices, a dark room full of whispering, rose and trailed away.

Deep shadows hung out over the green water. Flies circled in an isolated shaft of sunlight. James found it hard to move. He felt drowsy. He stopped backing away. The water swirled and eddied, forming strange back currents. Sunlight, shining on its surface, sparkled and then began to fade, as if a cloud had found its way across the sun.

James saw a shivering in the branches before him. Unseen birds began singing with savage abandon. Whole sections of foliage trembled, coming along from his left. A gnarled hand fell on his shoulder. It was the old man, McCollough. James clearly saw the inside of a house. Hundreds of empty cans, rusting. A cot, an old woman standing on a fence post like a bird, her arms flapping wildly, her eyes streaming blood. James saw an open field strewn with the corpses of dogs, dozens of dogs, blood staining the moonlit grass.

"Get the hell away from here!" McCollough screamed. He spun James around and using his free hand, dragged him up the slope with surprising strength. In his other hand, the old man carried a scarred black shotgun. He pulled James over the top of the steep bank and through the trees toward the open fields. James felt the shotgun shells in the old man's coat pocket slap against him as he was yanked stumbling along. There was a strong scent, a mix of sweat and cigarettes. He struggled to turn and look back toward the creek.

McCollough spun him around and taking him by the collar, slapped him. The blow woke James out of a half-dream to the horrors about him. McCollough's shirt was covered in blood. But there was much more. Something looming. The hairs on the back of James' neck twisted and stung. A coldness filled his chest.

"Swim here today, you swim here forever!" McCollough yelled. His eyes were wide and rimmed in yellow. Breathless, the old man drove him backwards. James fell, still gripping his rifle.

"You don't know what the hell you've stirred up here!" McCollough screamed. "Run!"

James leapt to his feet. He tore through the last few yards of underbrush and out into the open field. The sunlight was dazzling. He spun on his heel and stared back the way he had come but McCollough was already crashing back into the tree line toward the creek. The foliage closed on the old man, trembled, and then was still. In the silence, a shotgun blast rang out. James threw his hands up before his face, but the muffled shot had been fired down near the water. Dogs began to bay from various spots along the near bank.

A voice rose, high pitched and ragged.

"Run!"

James turned and ran. Again, the shotgun blast rang out. He ran towards the distant Wilson house, shimmering in the growing heat of late morning.

The boys walked along the bank of the creek. The air was still, the surrounding woods strangely silent. Mike called from behind. "What's that?"

They looked back upstream, the way they had come. A rising surge of water appeared around a distant turn. A single foaming wave was churning down the creek, pushing water up a foot against the dry bank. The wave approached and moved on by. The boys saw hundreds of silver shapes struggling in the water. It was a wave of fish. Catfish, carp, and big gar passed by, churning through the green water, their silver bellies flashing as they raced forward. They swept past and disappeared around a distant turn in the creek.

The boys looked at each other and back at the choppy water receding against the banks of the creek. It settled and grew still.

"What the hell was that all about?" Mike said.

"Hell if I know," Warren replied. He took off his glasses and wiped the lenses on his shirt. "Must be something in the creek," he said, looking back the way they had come. From that direction, a shotgun boomed once, and then again, a few moments later. The boys looked at each other and began hurrying back to where they had left James. When they arrived, the area was deserted, so they returned somewhat nervously to the house. When they got there, they found James sitting on the front step.

"Why didn't you come find us?" Warren said, exasperated.

"I tried," James said, still looking down.

"We were just up the creek," Warren said peering at him. "Who fired a shotgun?"

"I don't know," James said. He was visibly trembling.

"We had to come back here for nothing," Kevin said and went into the house.

"Let's get some lunch," Warren said following Kevin. James rose and followed the boys in, silently swearing not to let Kevin run him off again.

Chapter 5: Gone Crazy

The narrow low water bridge crossing Plum Creek was built of wooden beams. A single car could cross at a time. The boys lay on their backs on the bridge, looking up at patches of the afternoon sky visible through the leaves overhead. While there, they saw only one car: a long blue Oldsmobile driven by an old man. The boys rose and stood to the side of the road, making room for it to pass onto the narrow bridge. Warren put on a proprietary air, waving as they passed. The old man glanced over and raised one gnarled hand. The car disappeared over the rise into the afternoon glare, leaving a trail of white dust.

Warren said, "Let's go get a drink of water."

"Yeah," Mike said who had spit himself dry.

The boys left the shade of the trees and hiked up into the blazing sunshine. They walked along the white shale county road that led from the bridge which, after paralleling the creek a way, turned right and continued for half a mile or so, bringing them to a gate and cattle guard on their left. The gate was locked, blocking a smaller dirt road that disappeared around a turn. The heat was oppressive.

"Dad's gone," Warren said. He climbed the fence and jumped down on the far side. The others followed.

"This used to be the McCollough family farm,"

Warren said.

They walked for a half-mile or so along the sloping two track dirt road. Ahead, just visible above the trees, James saw the gray tin blades of a windmill slowly rotating in the shimmering afternoon light. Beneath it was a big round cement cistern.

The boys passed over a cattle guard into the yard and stood at the water cistern. Warren removed his hat and splashed water across his face. James studied the cistern. It was easily twenty-five feet across, the water three feet deep and clear. The inner sides below water level were coated with a thick growth of green algae. The water sparkled in the sunlight. He dipped his hands in and brought the cold water to his face.

A cable ran down from the top of the windmill. As the blades turned the cable rose and fell slowly, disappearing into a vertical pipe at the center of the windmill's base. Water pumped from deep in the earth spilled from a second pipe that extended over the side of the cistern. The boys took turns drinking directly from the pipe.

Mike looked up at James gasping. "You'll get used to the taste. It's the same all over Luling."

"Warren!" Kevin called out. He was a few yards away looking out across the heavily wooded hillside. Warren walked to where Kevin stood.

"What's burning?" Kevin asked. He pointed. A dark swell of smoke rose beyond the trees.

"I don't know," Warren said putting a hand on his hip. As he looked, another large billow of smoke rose. It was a deeper gray. The fire was growing. "Maybe Dad's burning brush?" Warren said shading his eyes.

The other boys were splashing each other by the cistern.

"C'mon!" Warren yelled.

They set off single file along a cow path through the thick underbrush. Then they turned up a steep grade through thickets of mesquite trees. Spider webs hung across the path, dragging sticky webs across their arms and faces. Warren snapped off a branch and used it to clear the webs out of the path as he walked. The others followed suit. After a few minutes, they headed even more steeply uphill. Mike swatted Sam with his branch from behind. Sam turned and kicked him in the thigh. Mike dropped the old single shot .22 and quickly picked it up as Warren turned around from the front of the line.

"Don't be so stupid," Warren snapped.

"What's the damn problem?" Sam asked.

"It's way too dry for a brush fire. The whole hillside could burn," Warren replied.

"Oh," said Sam.

The boys, hurrying along, fell silent. They skirted a ravine and disappeared into the sweltering underbrush.

"He's gone crazy," Warren whispered. "He's trying to burn the Hanging Tree."

The boys were crouched at the edge of a clearing. Before them, across the width of the open field, a fire burned beneath a towering oak. McCollough had piled logs and brush high around the base of the tree. As they watched, the smoke flared into the oak's upper limbs propelled by rising updrafts. Bursts of flames raced through the leaves crackling loudly. Beyond the blazing fire, the old man stood, half obscured by the shimmering heat waves. The heat distortions made him look skeletal, his thin arms waving wildly as the smoke rolled up into the afternoon light.

The old man was screaming. They could only hear bits and pieces of what he was yelling as his ragged voice rose and fell. Then, he disappeared behind the tree. His voice, fading in and out in the distance, surreal in the still afternoon air.

"What's he saying?" Mike asked.

"Shut up so maybe we can hear." Kevin replied.

James' heart was racing. He had told the boys nothing about encountering McCollough by the creek, and he meant to keep it that way, fearful his own standing would be damaged further simply by association.

"He's drunk," Mike said.

"If that tree catches, we'll never put it out," Warren said. "He carries a shot gun. And he's got those dogs, too. Must be thirty of em." He continued to watch for McCollough.

"He needs to be locked up," Kevin said.

None of the boys moved. Minutes passed. "I think he's gone," Warren said. The only sound they could hear was the distant crackling of the fire.

"Is he?" Mike said.

"I don't see him," Warren said.

"He's gone," James said.

"What the hell do you know?" Kevin said, turning with startling ferocity on James, but Warren broke from cover and began running toward the fire. The rest of the boys hesitated and then followed. Yards ahead, Warren ran wide-eyed with fear. The big oak tree rose towering into the sky above him. He clenched his teeth, ready to turn back if the old man appeared, but McCollough was nowhere in sight. Warren sprinted across the final twenty yards and dropped his rifle. He dashed in under the massive limbs and kicked at the burning logs.

"Knock down the fire!" Warren yelled.

"It's too hot!" Mike shouted back shielding his face from the blaze.

"Knock it down!" Warren repeated.

Kevin kicked at the burning limbs that leaned up against the thick trunk. A mass of hastily erected timbers collapsed across each other and rolled away from the tree.

"It's getting away!" James yelled. He stood to one side stamping at a grass fire that was threatening to spread into the open field. Sam ran to him, and they stamped out the flames that raced through the dry yellow grass. Embers spiraled into the blue sky, drifting away over the field. A dozen small fires leapt up as the boys ran from place-to-place stamping at the bright hot flames.

Kevin and Warren forced the burning logs away from the trunk. The shaded space under the tree's great limbs was like a furnace. As the logs fell away, smoke rose in whirling columns. The ground level became choked with an impenetrable bank of gray smoke.

Warren lost all sense of direction. He heard voices, other boys coughing. He held his shirt up to his face and breathed through it, listening for the sound of the fire, confused. Near his feet, he saw the dull orange glow of flames on every side. He took a step and felt the heat intensify. He stepped back again.

"Kevin!" he yelled.

"We got to get out of here." Kevin's voice was distant.

"We need wind!" Warren yelled.

Standing a few feet away, James felt a shock rising on his scalp. He looked up through the dense smoke in the limbs of the tree above him. For a moment, a great weight bore down on him; the sounds around him fading, muffled, then, the weight was gone. A strong breeze rippled the boys' clothes. It swept through the enclosed space beneath the tree, driving the smoke before it, clearing the air.

With a little more effort, they finally brought the fire under control. They stood by, sweat pouring down their faces. Wisps of smoke still drifted in a haze beneath the sheltering branches of the tree. Late afternoon sunlight shone down through the oak's gnarled limbs. Ash and dust turned slowly in the updraft.

They examined the oak, James fully realizing how big and how very old the tree was. Its trunk leaned slightly, holding up massive limbs, which hung out parallel to the ground for dozens of yards in every direction.

The fire had singed the great branches toward the center of the tree. Long swaths of the trunk were charred black. Pale drops of sap were already forming across the bottom of the lower limbs where the rising flames had struck head on. A faint hissing could be heard as steam escaped.

Kevin took out a cigarette. "Got a light?" he joked.

The boys were grinning like idiots, their clothes and faces dirty with long streaks of ash. For a moment, James felt himself part of the group. He knew the feeling wouldn't last long, but for a moment he let himself imagine being one of them.

Chapter 6: A Night Swim

The boys sat in the den. Sunlight streamed in though the big plate glass window. The air conditioner droned in one of the windows alongside the fireplace. Outside on the driveway, the old ranch truck was parked behind Mr. Wilson's Buick. The boys ate their dinner, BBQ sandwiches Mr. Wilson had brought from town. Mr. Wilson was in the kitchen cleaning up.

Each of the boys had a short stack of comic books to read during the meal. Sam reached over and took a cookie from a bag next to him on the couch. He spoke without taking his eyes from the comic book in his hands.

"You know, Warren, these are the worst comic books ever," Sam said. He turned a page and munched his cookie.

"So, don't read em," Warren said.

"Where'd you get this many Richie Rich comics anyway?" Sam continued.

"They were Peggy's," Warren said. He turned the page and settled deeper in his chair, one leg slug over the arm.

"So, why not bring some better ones?" Mike said.

Warren put down his comic book and looked at Mike. "I like Richie Rich." he said.

"You are Richie Rich," Sam said under his breath.

They read for a while.

"We'll head back down to the creek tonight," Warren said. Already outside the sun was angling down, throwing rich golden light along the wall of the den.

James sat upright. He looked at Warren in genuine disbelief. "You don't really go to the creek at night."

"Ha! Chicken," Kevin said loudly.

"What are you worried about? We have flashlights," Mike said.

"What about snakes?" James said.

"What about snakes?" Mike replied. "That's why we go at night. We're hunting them."

James sat for a moment, wrestling with a combination of embarrassment and alarm. He struggled for something else to say. "Why is that tree called a Hanging Tree?" he said.

"Cuz that's what it is." Warren said.

"No way," James said.

"Dad!" Warren said loudly to his father in the kitchen. "Is the tree McCollough tried to burn, a hanging tree?"

"It is, yes," Mr. Wilson replied from the kitchen. The water tap was turned off. Mr. Wilson appeared in the doorway.

"How long ago was it… I mean…?" James' voice trailed off.

"My father says he saw two men executed there when he was a boy, around 1910. They were convicted of killing a bank clerk in Seguin. That old path that runs next to it was the road to Seguin."

James' mind was racing.

"After those two, they stopped executions here, and sent them instead over to the new county prison in Lockhart," Mr. Wilson said. He picked up his set of car keys from the top of a small table. "Warren, I'm going into town to see your grandfather."

"Yes, sir," Warren replied.

"Stay away from McCollough's place. Stay on our property this side of the low water bridge, you understand?" Mr. Wilson said.

"Yes, sir," Warren replied.

Mr. Wilson pulled the door to behind him. The truck started and backed out of the driveway.

"What are we gonna do out there?" James asked.

"We already told you," said Warren sounding irritable.

"But we'll get bit," James said, a strange conviction rising in him.

"If you're worried about getting bit, you shouldn't be wearing sneakers," Warren said.

James looked at the others.

"We're going to the creek," Kevin said, smiling faintly.

"What about McCollough?" James said, aware that his voice was rising in pitch. "Maybe we should stay around here. We could shoot bottle rockets."

All four boys were now looking at James. Sam's mouth hung open. "What are you talking about? We always go hunting at night," he said. "There's more stuff out."

Mike was more sympathetic, "I could shoot fireworks."

Kevin smiled. "Warren and I are going to the creek. You guys can go with us or stay here with Jimmy." And there it was. Plain and simple.

"McCollough's wandering around out there," James insisted, trying yet again.

Warren finally said flatly, "If you're scared you can stay here, Jimmy." He went back to reading. One by one the others did the same.

Kevin got up and walked over to the bag of cookies by Sam. He took three and dropped one in Sam's lap on the way back to his chair. A contented silence fell over most of the group. Sam chewed his cookie meditatively as he read his comic book. Finally, he let out a long sigh.

"Hey, Warren," he said. "Would you autograph my Richie Rich comic book?"

The moon rose early in a clear sky. The night air was warm. The boys crossed the highway and passed through the barbed wire fence beyond. They passed the white barn on the hilltop as they had done earlier in the day. Its big tin covered doors were closed. Now they could see a single tungsten floodlight mounted high on a pole which lit the front of the barn. They headed down the cow path through the heavily wooded hillside to the darkened fields beyond.

Warren was in the lead with a flashlight, his pistol on his belt. Now that it was dark, he had left his rifle at home. Behind him, the rest of the boys trailed along single file. Kevin carried the Remington shotgun and a second flashlight. Sam carried the small .410 shotgun. The last two boys carried nothing.

As edgy as being out in the dark made him, James was not going to be left alone again. The darkened landscape was alive with subtle sounds of night life. The boys stopped and listened to a loud noise in the bushes. Something was scrabbling away into the thick underbrush.

"Armadillo," Warren said. "They don't care how much noise they make."

They had walked this same route earlier that day. They again passed the tiny pond. Its surface still, mirroring the sky overhead, its gray mud banks pock marked with hoof prints, lunar in the moonlight. James thought of the bullfrog Warren had shot earlier, now sunk in the mud at the bottom of the pond, its belly a pale white smear in the blackness.

As they reached the bottom of the hill, the field opened

before them. It seemed vast at night. Warren turned onto a new cow path and headed towards the far side. To their left, in the distance, were the pillars of the highway 90 overpass, which towered above the expansive bottomland of the creek. Warren and Kevin whipped their flashlight beams about, across the trail and out towards the trees, seeking telltale reflections of animal eyes in the distance. Eventually Warren switched off his flashlight and then Kevin did the same.

"The moon's bright enough, we don't need em," Warren said in a low voice. With the lights off, James saw the ground at his feet disappear into darkness.

"Aw c'mon guys. Turn the flashlights back on," he said.

"Shut up, Jimmy," Kevin said not looking back.

"Turn em on," James said his panic rising.

No one responded.

They continued to walk single file. James desperately tried to control the fear roiling in his gut. Crossing the field, the boys approached the towering bulk of the Hanging Tree. The full moon, still rising, was tangled in the upper branches. The great limbs of the tree glowed silver and gray. A few embers glowed. Wisps of smoke hung in the branches, unwilling to mix with the clean night air. In the distance, an owl called. It had a mournful plaintive sound. They stopped before the tree. The moonlight could not penetrate the oak's great canopy of leaves. It was dark beneath.

"We're gonna have to send that old man to the funny farm," Warren said to no one in particular.

"Can I have a flashlight?" James said loudly.

Kevin spun on his heel, walked over to James, and switching his flashlight on, shone the beam directly in James' face. "Jimmy, we didn't bring you along to listen to you whine all night."

Kevin side-stepped James and swept the thinner boy's legs from beneath him. James fell heavily then scrambled back to his feet. Mike and Sam stood silent. Warren waited and watched.

"I mean it, Jimmy. Shut up," Kevin said. He tossed James the flashlight. It hit James in the hands and fell to the ground. James quickly found it and switched it on.

Kevin walked back up to where Warren stood.

"I told you he'd start up," Kevin said.

"He's your cousin," Warren replied. They continued past the tree. Sam followed them.

Mike gave Jimmy a pat on the arm and shrugged. James shone the beam of light down by his feet.

"Thanks for the flashlight," he said loudly, shame and anger mixing equally.

Kevin lit a cigarette. He tossed the lit match away into the grass, daring Warren to say something. The small flame sputtered and went out. After a short while, they reached another path heading uphill and disappeared among the stunted mesquites.

The boys stood in darkness along the bank of the creek. Kevin puffed slowly on his cigarette, the shotgun across the crook of his arm. Warren was down on one knee with his pistol out. Mike and James trained the flashlights on a spot at midstream fifteen feet below them. They remained silent, watching the single illuminated patch of water. The center was bright yellow, moving toward green at the edge and then pitch black.

James felt his gut coiling tight as a drum. He tried to relax, exhaling slowly. Away from the light, they heard a slap in the water.

"Keep it there," Warren said quietly.

James and Sam continued to point the flashlights at the point midstream. A shadow passed beneath the lit patch of water. James heard Warren pull back the hammer on the .38. The shadow passed again beneath the patch of light, this time much more substantial. The shape grew clearer, finally solid. He saw the long snout of a gar gently ease into the light. A single black eye rolled past, followed by gleaming scales and a fin. The fish was over three feet long. A single dorsal fin gently slid past.

The boom of the .38 was deafening. Water leapt up dead center on the patch of light. The fish showed its bright white belly. It turned over in the water, a red stain encircling it, and then dropped slowly away, a single eye staring, growing faint, gone.

James quickly shone his flashlight about him, first at the ground near his feet, then across the nearby trees. A procession of brown and gray trunks flashed past.

"Good shot," Kevin said.

Warren put the pistol in his holster.

Sam had moved around behind James, a lit cigarette in his hand. A bottle rocket exploded into life beneath James' feet.

James hollered. He spun away from the geyser of colored sparks, slipped off the top of the bank, white spots dancing before his eyes. He landed hard and tumbled part way down the incline. Clutching for a handful of brush, he managed to stop his fall, belly down, a foot above the dark water. The flashlight rolled past. He heard a splash as it hit the water and disappeared. Stealing a look over his shoulder, he saw the flashlight's glow from deep beneath the water. Something wriggled by in the dull green light. Then, it winked out. Another flashlight beam was in his face.

"You lost my flashlight," Warren said from behind the

bright light.

"I'm sliding," James said from between his teeth. "Help me!" He started to rise, grabbing for another handful of weeds, and felt them give. With that, he was in the water. He felt the cold shock first on his face and hands and then through his clothes across his back and legs and his feet within his sneakers. He struggled to stand, lifting his face out of the water. He felt something slide up against his leg. In a flash, he was clawing at the bank, blinded by water and mud.

"Oh, god!" James yelled.

"Take a hold of my hand," Kevin shouted.

The flashlight beam was still in his eyes. Before him, Kevin stood, feet dug into the bank at an angle. James took hold of the hand and struggled to rise out of the water up the slick mud and clay of the bank.

Again, he felt something sinuous moving against his ankle.

"...your feet in sideways," Kevin yelled at him.

Water in his eyes and ears, James rose partly out of the creek. Kevin's firm grip on his hand slipped a little.

"Dig your feet in sideways, you dumb ass!" Kevin yelled.

James felt the hand give completely and again he was beneath the dark water. He fought to gain his balance. *Get out of the water, right now.* James rose, struggling and again took Kevin's outstretched hand.

"...sideways!" Warren was also yelling at him.

James dug the sides of his feet into the slippery mud and struggled up out of the water. His ears cleared and he could hear again. He half climbed and was half dragged up the steep incline. As the ground grew dry, he let go of Kevin's hand, dropped to all fours, and scrambled up the rest of the way.

James crawled onto level ground heaving for breath. "What the hell did you do that for!" He stood shakily, glaring at Sam.

"I didn't tell you to jump in the creek, man," Sam said taking a step back, his hands raised.

"Screw you! Screw all of you!" James yelled. Mud covered his forearms and the side of his face. "What an asshole thing to do," he sputtered. He tried to shake some of the mud off his hands.

"Don't mess with him anymore, you scared me half to death," Mike pleaded. Warren continued to hold the flashlight beam on James.

"You're okay Jimmy," Warren said, venturing closer.

"I'm great," James replied bitterly.

They all stared at him, a little embarrassed. James looked down at his clothes. The tension faded and the boys began to giggle.

"Sorry, man," Sam said, smiling.

James scraped a clump of mud off his knee and stepped toward Sam with it. He wiped a smear of mud on the front of Sam's shirt. "There you go, Sam," he said.

"After all that talk about snakes." Mike said also smiling.

James paused. "I could feel them in the water." His face clouded. He turned to Kevin. "Thanks for getting me out," he said.

Kevin lit a cigarette and watched his cousin.

"Sorry, I lost the flashlight," James said. He turned to look back down at the dark water.

"It's all right," Warren said. "We have more. We'll go back to the house and change your clothes."

Warren turned and there before them, stood McCollough, illuminated in the harsh light of the flashlight. He pushed Warren back roughly and swung his shotgun up to point at the boys. McCollough's face was battered and swollen; his eyes deeply rimmed in red. The old man rubbed his sleeve across his mouth. Clumps of dirt fell to the ground.

"Why'd you put my fire out?" he said. They stood silently watching the tip of the shotgun barrel as it waved slowly left and right before them.

"Why'd you put my damned fire out!" he yelled. "Why didn't you let that damned tree burn? We could 'a lived!" he barked. He took a halting step toward them.

"Mr. McCollough, sir, this here is my family's property; since 1967..," Warren began haltingly.

McCollough spat. "You boys picked a hell of a night to be out pissing around in these woods." He wiped his lips again. His hands were stained dark red. Warren dropped the light a few inches. McCollough's shirt and pants were soaked in blood.

"Oh, my god," Mike whispered.

Beside McCollough, a big dirty white dog appeared. Its tongue hung down. It was panting, dull rasping pants of exhaustion. McCollough put one hand on the dog's head. "Your kin will set up a terrible wailing with you boys gone," McCollough said flatly.

"What does he mean?" Sam asked in a harsh whisper.

"He come for the dogs last night. Now he's come for me," McCollough murmured, his attention wavering from the boys. "Bad night. You picked a bad night."

"Oh, Jesus... ," James murmured.

"Jesus?" McCollough said loudly, his attention focusing on James. He stepped towards the boy.

"Jesus, you say?" McCollough reached out a blood-soaked hand and took James by the collar. "Jesus!" the old man spit the word in James' face. "Jesus ain't troubled himself with these here parts for nigh on one hundred years.

He got no truck with us here, boy. He got no business!"
McCollough drew James' face to within inches of his own.
His breath stank of rot and alcohol. The boy's eyes were
wide with terror.

McCollough's voice became a flat, heated whisper.
"You got no idea what's walking these fields. But I'll tell
you this, YOU stirred him up." The old man looked for a
long moment at James trembling before him.

"You got the mark on you, boy. Death is leaning over
your shoulder." He slowly put the shotgun barrel to James'
throat. "I'd be doing you a favor to take your head off right
now," he said. James closed his eyes. His lips began to
move quickly in the Lord's Prayer. He rushed to finish it.

The old man's eyes went blank. He pushed James to
the ground and turned to face the others. He saw that Kevin
had his shotgun up and pointed. Warren stood by his pistol
half drawn, uncertain of what to do.

McCollough's eyes grew narrow. "Hanged Man never
came all the way out of the shadows until that one come
here! Woke the Hanged Man up. Called him all the way into
the world!" He pointed to the creek. "The trap is already
sprung." He let out a barking ugly laugh. He pointed at
James. "Your little friend here is waking up nightmares.
Stirring them up!"

McCollough's voice rose, torn ragged by exhaustion.
"Run for home you little bastards! Run every way like
rabbits. See what good it does ya. Hanged Man's coming
for us all tonight!"

A crackle of distant thunder sounded. It was followed
by a second, much closer. The grove was lit in blue light.
The old man again pointed to the creek. "Look!"

Warren turned his flashlight towards the creek. A flash
of lightning lit the surface; now up by twenty feet, level to
the top of the bank. Dark roiling water now covered the

space to the far side. It had become a raging river. Warren turned back. McCollough was already disappearing through the trees.

"Where's all the blood from?" Sam asked.

"He's killing his dogs?" Mike ventured, confused.

James frantically tried to wipe the blood from his shirt. Looking at the red on his hands, he gagged, choking on acid and bile.

"Let's get out of here," Kevin said.

"Wait! Don't run out into the open," Warren said. "Let him get out of range."

The boys moved to the edge of the tree line. Although the lightning played wildly along the horizon, the air remained still. McCollough and his dog were hurrying across the moonlit field. The figure of the old man swayed side to side as he ran. The distant lightning flashed, turning the night to day. Then it was dark again. The figures became more distant in the moonlight, blending in with the line of trees.

"There must be flash flooding up stream," Warren said, glancing back at the creek raging behind them. He turned back to peer out into the field. He had turned off the flashlight and tucked it into his belt. It was eerily silent. Bursts of heat lightning lit the field, illuminating the stillness. A breeze began to rise. When the lightning came again, there was a third figure in the distance.

"Let's go," Kevin said. He took Warren's arm and started to walk. They saw a muzzle flash in the distance. The sound of the shotgun echoed across the open space. It was followed by the sharp piercing cry of a dog. James felt the hairs on the back of his neck standing up.

"He's shooting the dog," Warren said.

"No, he ain't," James said.

A second shot come rolling across the field. The

howling ended.

"He damn well did shoot the dog," Kevin said. "Let's get the hell out of here!"

"He isn't alone," Warren said, pointing.

"To hell with this," Kevin said, and he was bolting away across the open field. Mike reflexively ran after Kevin. The other boys hesitated. As Kevin and Mike disappeared into the distance, two other figures could be seen moving towards the remaining boys from across the field. The rising breeze brought a hint of rot. McCollough and something else were locked in an eerie embrace, moving slowly in a long, graceful arc across the field. It was a bleak and stumbling pirouette. There were subtle indications of a fading one-sided struggle.

As they got closer, the bright moonlight began to pick out details. James felt an immense exhaustion sweeping towards him from across the field. He closed his eyes. He felt a coolness rise through his gut to touch his beating heart. He felt the stars wink out, one by one. He raised his head and forced his eyes open.

James could just make out the figure of McCollough being dragged by someone or something. It held McCollough by his throat and pulled him lazily across the ground, the old man's legs hung limp. McCollough's head was back, bent at a contorted angle. He was not struggling. In the eerie silence, the boys heard a damp pop, like cornstalks being bent double, and McCollough struck the dry earth, a last shuddering sigh leaving him.

The distant figure turned to face their way. A terrible thrill struck James. It was hanging in midair; floating at least a foot off the ground, its boot tips drifting across the tips of the long grass. Its head was topped by a shock of white hair, framed by the great disk of the moon. A flicker of lightning flashed low along the horizon.

The distant apparition began to move again. It turned in graceful drifting circles that grew increasingly larger. It was turning round and round in the field. A star fell across the sky above, a single thin line of pure white light. The lightning grew suddenly in intensity, dark clouds sweeping up, erupting on every side, flashing hot and bright all about them. The clouds closed in, covered the moon, plunging the field into darkness. A strong wind picked up, shaking the trees about them. James felt a swarming pressure in his head.

"It's coming," James shouted. Another flicker of lightning confirmed this. For an instant, he saw the ragged figure racing forward, its white hair trailing, a dark "O" for its mouth. James turned and looked toward the creek, the buzzing in his head growing.

Along the bank, thousands of snakes wriggled in the hard pools of illumination that flashed down through the leaves. Snakes were swarming out of the floodwaters onto the dry land. The woods grew bright as day. The thunder was deafening. The snakes spilled down from the top of the bank toward them. A single long shape coiled before James. He yelled.

As the boys turned, the snake struck James. In the brilliant light, Warren saw the snake hanging from James' pants leg. It was tattered and half rotten. James kicked wildly at it with his free foot, tearing the serpent in two. His eyes showed white all around. He rose and bolted away along the path through the trees. Warren raced after him with Sam close behind.

The Hanged Man slowed to a stop. Figures scattered through the woods and across the fields; flushed out from hiding. The flow of water pulled magnetic, left to right. Lightning, sharp like bristles, danced along the tops of the trees. The Hanged Man strained to exhale a slow bubbling breath of rotting air; struggled to pass the breath through a broken neck and crushed esophagus. It felt the boys' fear sweet and strong. Straining, the Hanged Man blew forth a spew of rot and foul air, its head lolling from side to side. With the breath came a word, barked out hoarsely past rigid lips; lips pulled back off teeth in a long grimace.

"Hatch," the Hanged Man said.

A clean high-level wind tore at the great clouds above the field, revealing the bright face of the moon. The field was empty, save for McCollough who lay mute and spent, his dead eyes staring upward into the night sky.

Chapter 7: On the Run

Warren concentrated on catching James. He quickly outpaced Sam. Warren began reciting the steps for treating snakebite under his breath as he ran. He ducked an oncoming branch and, weaving left and right, ran as fast as he could down the path. He heard a crash in the woods ahead and slightly to his right.

"Jimmy!" he yelled. He knew that James was spreading the venom as he ran.

A flash of lightning revealed a figure dashing through the trees off the trail. He gritted his teeth and pounded after him.

Better be Jimmy, he thought.

James ran wildly through the darkness ahead. Patches of moonlight appeared. Twice he slammed hard into a broad trunk, scrambled to his feet, and bolted on.

Occasionally, his feet splashed through rising water, and he would veer right. He caught glimpses of strange figures drifting through the trees. Branches slashed at his face and arms. Behind him, Warren yelled his name, but it was useless. He neither heard nor understood.

Kevin held up. After running blindly for long minutes, he spun around to get his bearings. In the moonlight he saw only the long grass and stunted mesquite trees spreading out on all sides.

He hastily checked his pockets for shotgun shells, counting them by touch. He removed a shell and, flipping over the Remington, tried to shove it into the magazine. It wouldn't go. The gun was fully loaded. He flipped the gun back over and bobbling the shell, dropped it to the ground.

He dropped to his knees and searched the ground in the dark. He heard someone or something running towards him from the direction he had just come. He stood and flipped the safety off on the shotgun.

Warren charged after the fleeing figure before him. They seemed to have passed beyond the snakes. Lightning flickered illuminating the trees. Out of the semi-darkness, a tree limb lashed him across his mouth and throat. The pain turned to anger. As they ran, James angled away and Warren cut through the trees to intercept him. The two collided. Warren took hold of the James and struggled to turn him around.

"Jimmy, god dammit, it's me!" he yelled. "It's Warren, now hold still. You're bit!" James lashed out wildly, his hands clawed at Warren's face and chest. A flash of lightning lit the woods. Warren saw James' face, wild eyed and contorted horribly. The boy's lips were pulled back, showing blood-flecked teeth. He had bitten through part of his tongue. James' struggles were growing fiercer. His hands found their way towards Warren's throat.

Warren looped his arm around James' neck in a half nelson. He threw his hip into the thinner boy's body and pulling James across his leg, thumped him brutally against the ground, then sat on him. James was silent. Warren listened intently to the woods as James' struggled weakly beneath him.

"Jimmy, I'm gonna get off you now and fix your bite. If you start fighting me again, I'm gonna knock the hell out you; you hear me?" Warren hissed, peering down at the boy.

James moaned slightly. Warren pulled the flashlight loose from his belt. He cupped the light with his hand and showed a narrow beam on James' face. The boy was no longer conscious. A large ugly bruise was rising all along the side of his head from where he had collided with a tree. Blood ran from his nose and along his neck from his ear. His skin was whitish and pale from shock, either from the venom or the ugly head wound. In the distance, Warren heard the dull boom of a shotgun.

"Shit," he muttered as he pulled up James' pants leg. It would only come part way. Warren unsnapped the knife from his belt and slipped the sharp blade under the fabric of James' pants. He succeeded in cutting through the thick denim. He laid back the cloth and turned on the flashlight. There, halfway up James' calf were two slender red wounds.

"Aw, Jimmy," Warren muttered. He used the loose material of the pants to wipe the wound. Then he popped open the small pouch on his belt and feeling around among the .38 shells fished out a kitchen match. He struck the match on the handle of his knife and ran the blade a few times back and forth through the bright flame. Glancing at James face, he cut a broad slash across the snakebite wound. The flesh parted evenly. Warren felt himself growing nauseous. He looked away and drew the knife across the wound again, making a red X. Sour bile rose in his mouth. The match sputtered out. Warren hesitated for a moment longer and then placing his lips on the wound, sucked out blood and venom, and spit it against the base of a nearby tree. He repeated the process three or four times and then searched about for a bandage. He chose to cut a strip off his shirt and used it to bind the wound, keeping the fabric in a broad band across the place where he had made the cuts.

"Even pressure, even pressure," he murmured under his breath. Then he quickly switched off the flashlight. His hands were shaking. He fell back to rest. Lightning flickered weakly though the trees, outlining the limbs above him. He sat up with a start. Someone was whispering to him.

"Mister," the voice said.

Warren drew his pistol and turned.

"Who's there," Warren hissed.

A wind rippled through the trees. A figure moved forward, his face in deep shadow.

"Don't come any closer," Warren said. The gun in his hand was shaking.

The figure in the trees raised his hands, palms out. "Just looking for the way out of these woods," he said.

"You're trespassing," Warren said.

"He knows the way out," the man said, pointing towards James.

A breeze rose, and the figure was gone.

"Warren," a different voice said. It was Sam.

"Over here," Warren said.

Sam crept up through the trees. He began to pass by to the left.

"Here," Warren repeated.

Sam turned and came into the small clearing. He sat heavily on the ground. He didn't speak. His jaw worked slowly side to side. His breath rose and fell in the stillness.

"James got snake bit," Warren said. He showed the flashlight beam in a narrow slit between his fingers. James was on his side, his legs splayed open.

"I guess he knew what he was talking about after all,"

Sam said ruefully. "Where's Kevin and Mike?" His voice cracked slightly.

"They're long gone," Warren said. He exhaled loudly. "You hear the shot gun?"

"Yeah," Sam said. Neither boy wanted to suggest what that might mean.

The two boys crouched over James. They turned him fully onto his back, straightening his arms.

"What happened to his face," Sam said, bending closer.

"Ran into a tree," Warren said.

The two boys remained quiet for a moment.

"We gotta get out of here," Sam said. He peered down at James' face in the semi-darkness. James muttered, his head turning slowly side-to-side.

"We can't leave him, and we can't take him with us. One of us has to go for help," Warren said.

Kevin and Mike crouched side by side in the field. Before them, the open space stretched out still and quiet. The opposite tree line appeared as a long low wall of dark forms that rose along the hillside. To their right, the elevated highway ran 50 feet above the ground level in the distance crossing the flood plain that ran along the creek.

"I'm telling you, that's the fastest way," Kevin continued, pointing across the open field to the tree covered hillside beyond.

"That's too far," Mike whispered, growing frantic.

"We'll find the path," Kevin said.

"Do you see one?" Mike replied. "Do you see anything?"

"Listen to me," Kevin replied. "If we cross straight over, we get to the barn. After that, it's straight down to the house."

Mike pleaded. "Look, it's right there. Somebody'll pick us up." He pointed toward the highway gleaming in the distance.

"I'm going straight across," Kevin said. He shifted the shotgun to his right hand and stood.

"Kevin, wait a minute," Mike said, grabbing him by the arm.

"What?" Kevin said angrily.

"Don't leave me," Mike said. His eyes were wide.

Kevin set the butt of the shotgun on the ground. "We're going that way and we're going now. Just haul ass."

Mike took a deep breath. "Do you see anything?" Mike said.

"No," Kevin said.

"You don't see anything?" Mike said.

"No, nothing," Kevin replied. He started walking.

"Don't leave me behind," Mike said from between his teeth. Kevin's long strides became a slow trot.

"So don't get left," Kevin said.

Kevin's speed increased. Mike raced along behind, desperate to keep pace. Bull nettle thorns slashed across his ankles. By the time they reached the halfway point to the hillside, Kevin was drawing away from him. The smaller boy, already ten or twelve paces behind, put his head down and pounded along behind. The fear in his belly turned to cold dread. Kevin was running full out, leaving the smaller boy behind. Mike cried out. It came out as a raspy croak. Overhead, the clouds fled as quickly as they had come. Stars were flung up by the thousands. The moon shone across the field. The grass at Mike's feet hissed by as he raced through it. He did not look back.

"Kevin!" Mike yelled. Kevin was nearly all the way to the tree line, Mike looked right and left as he ran. He saw no path up the hillside. It was pitch black within the tree line. The smaller boy's legs were growing numb and wobbly beneath him as he ran. There was a ringing in his ears.

Mike finally glanced back and saw it. The Hanged Man, racing up behind him like a torn flag in the wind; stark and white, the moon dangling above it; a cold halo. In the split second that Mike turned to glance, he saw moonlight reflect off a wet place in a shadowy mouth. He ran for his life.

The first trees were within reach. He felt the lightest touch against the side of his head. He tumbled forward and his hand struck a branch. He stumbled; rose; and plunged directly into the dark, dense foliage.

The steep hillside had never been bulldozed. The branches hung thick all the way to the ground. Mike did not feel the cactus thorns or bull nettle as they raked at his arms and face. He lunged uphill, seeing nothing in the darkness but the faintest hints of moonlight passing through the higher branches; small patches of blue light that rolled past him as he struggled upward in the close and airless dark.

He struck a small open space in the blackness and was suddenly clawing through a sea of moonlit spider webs. For a moment, he stopped, his breath coming in deep lunging gasps. Webs lay across his face. He felt them on his lips and eyelids; then the feathery touch of struggling forms; spiders hanging, momentarily trapped, their legs moving softly against him.

Mike screamed, clawing at the webs on his face, as he churned uphill through the thick underbrush. He fell and rose again, fighting wildly for every additional foot of progress. Abruptly, he found himself standing on clear ground at the top of the hill, the open air cool against his face. All terror fell away. A dull numbness took its place. He stood before the old white barn they had seen at a distance earlier in the day. Barbed wire fence and a gate stood across the way. Mounted on a pole in the middle of the yard was the bright tungsten floodlight. It buzzed softly, moths circling it. There was a single large oak next to it, casting an impenetrable shadow beneath it. Mike took a few steps, brushed a handful of webs off his arm and paused, standing on wobbly legs. He was cut and bleeding in a dozen places. Sweat poured off him. A gentle breeze rustled the leaves on the hilltop.

He heard a truck passing far off. He looked at the distant highway curving in a long arc right to left past the fence and the sloping fields beyond. It was no more than a quarter mile away. Alongside the highway, the windows of the Wilson ranch house glowed warmly.

Mike began to walk toward the distant house. His steps slowed and then stopped. He stood wavering slightly in the open yard. The house seemed dreamlike in the distance. He felt a deep relaxation creeping over him. The drone of night insects rose from the tall grass beyond the fence.

Behind Mike, the gaunt figure of the Hanged Man emerged silently from the shadows of the trees. It drifted across the open ground, its boot tips touching the top of the grass. It drew to a stop behind the small boy, moving gently from side to side. Its bound hands were at the level of the boy's throat. In the harsh glow of the light, the Hanged Man's stretched, broken throat pulsed and twitched in lurid detail, like a section of some immense reptile, giving no support to the creature's head which tilted wobbling and twitching along one shoulder.

On its otherwise expressionless face, the Hanged Man's mouth was a wet smear, the tongue dangling down its cheek; a loose dead thing, plastered with strands of its long dry hair that blew about weakly. The flesh of its face was white as chalk, pitted and utterly cold. Its eyes were black marbles, gleaming with the dull sheen of mucus in their darkened sockets.

Slowly its fingers settled on Mike's throat. The boy, half in a dream, almost in irritation, swatted at the hands. The Hanged Man drifted back a pace, its black eyes unmoving. It drifted forward to again take a purchase. The small boy's face grew slightly clouded as if he were back in school, trying to figure long division in his head.

From shadows alongside the barn a shotgun blast boomed.

"Mike! Run!" Kevin yelled, stepping into the light.

The shotgun blast snapped Mike out of the Hanged Man's spell. He lurched away from the horror behind him and ran across the yard. In the deep shadows beneath the tree in the center of the yard, a big water pump housing stood upright. Mike crashed against the upright metal housing. He fell to the ground, hit the back of his head, and lay for a moment looking up. The brightly lit green leaves overhead wobbled and ran like water down a windshield. And then it was dark.

Warren stood and shone his flashlight out across the field. He made three rhythmic sweeps and then crouched again.

"I wish you wouldn't keep doing that," Sam said.

"Dad may be trying to find us," Warren replied.

They had left James' side and were sitting a few feet away. Neither had been comfortable staying too close to the stricken boy. He had become a liability. The woods were silent except for the distant rushing of water in the creek. Warren was thinking about that thing McCollough had called the Hanged Man. It became less real with each passing moment. Surely McCollough wasn't lying dead out in the field. But then, Warren thought of the sound that McCollough's neck made. He knew every step of the way back to the house, but he was too afraid to get up and walk home. The fields of his ranch, just hours earlier, a place of unerring confidence for him, were now something deeply threatening and unfamiliar.

"Where are they?" Sam whispered.

Warren stirred and said, "They're headed for the house to get help."

"That's good, yeah…" Sam said.

"They might be there already," Warren added.

"Yeah, your Dad will be here soon," Sam said.

"Yeah," Warren said, but he wasn't entirely convinced. Even so, he listened for the sound of his father's ranch truck; coming across the fields to take them back to the house. They would call the police and bring them back to the field. Nobody gets away from the cops. That's a fact. The idea of police searching the field was comforting. He thought about that and waited. After a time, the dull boom of a distant shotgun blast drifted through the trees. Sam stood up.

They're not at the house, Warren thought. As best he could judge, it was coming from near the old barn.

Warren peered toward the shadowy figure of James lying a few feet away on the ground but didn't move to check on him. Sam had fallen silent. James' face was hidden in deep shadow, his breathing shallow and hoarse. The two boys remained at a distance from him. Warren knew snake venom generally wouldn't kill you unless you were allergic or very weak, but James was in bad shape, there was no denying it. He tried to forget that the shotgun had been fired. He waited, hoping for the sound of the ranch truck.

Mike opened his eyes and saw the tangle of bright leaves above his head. He felt nauseous. The leaves were lit day-glow green by the light post, like a stage set. *Is it night? Yes. It's night.* For a moment, he thought he was home in his bed and that this was one of those dreams inside a dream, but what had happened before the leaves he could not remember. It made him uneasy to think of it. He blinked, but the leaves remained, quivering slightly in the night breeze. Then he remembered the car ride from Houston. *Was that today? No, yesterday.* He sensed a curious blank spot between then and now. In a rush came memories of the tree and the fire that afternoon. Then he remembered leaving the ranch house that evening, walking along the creek with flashlights. Then, McCollough falling to the ground and the blackness of the wooded hillside. For a moment, the memory was without any associated emotion and then he fully remembered the flight through the woods.

He lay perfectly still, holding his breath now. *Something else...* he thought, and the final piece came to him. He remembered the cold hands on his neck. An ugly ripping chill ran through his guts. Terror moved to paralyze him. He stifled a gag reflex by clamping his jaws tight. The effort made his head throb painfully. Above, the bright green leaves continued to stir gently.

He closed his eyes, opened them, and inch by inch, raised himself up. Pain filled his head, a hot ember behind his eyes. Momentarily his vision was a wash of angry colors. Then the barn yard became visible through the haze. He rolled onto his shoulder and looked around him.

He saw the barn, illuminated by the light. To one side, there was the beginning of a dirt road that angled away into the darkness. Mike exhaled and took a deep breath. He gathered his feet under him into a crouch. He felt something warm running into his eyes. He brought his hand down. It was deep red with blood.

"Oh, man," he muttered, wiping his hand on the long grass. One of his legs gave way, pitching him forward. He rose again, struggling to remain upright.

He peered into the shadows. Another wave of nausea swept over him as he struggled and stood. A breeze rose. He rested one hand on the water pump housing next to him. *Where is Kevin?* he thought. The yard was completely empty. He looked past the fence toward the highway and the house beyond. He took a few steps toward the house, feeling stronger. He heard a sound in the tall grass beyond the fence. Something was crawling about through the undergrowth.

"Oh, c'mon…," Mike whined.

Whatever it was, it was between him and the warm lights of the house in the distance. A second thrashing erupted loudly to one side of the first. Mike stepped back a pace. He realized that movement was coming from all along the fence line. He heard sounds from beyond the small outbuildings to his left and right. Something rose in the deep shadows of the barn and shambled forward.

Mike gave a longing glance toward the house. He saw the warm yellow glow of the windows.

"Somebody, help us!" he screamed.

At the sound of his scream, the movement around him intensified. Moist grunting and coughing echoed. Only the way behind him was still not blocked.

Something four legged lumbered out into the light by the barn. Mike saw the motion of it out of the corner of his eye. He turned away, raising his hand to block the view of it. He broke from the yard, racing down the dirt road towards the open fields from which he had come.

Kevin crouched in the tall grass next to the white shale

country road they had walked earlier that day. The shotgun felt heavy, but he would not leave it behind while he had shells; and he had a lot of shells.

The road, he knew, led to the bridge, which was where he would find Warren but, how far from the bridge he was now, he could not say. The flight from the yard where Mike fell had been furious and blind. He could still see the terrible gaunt figure turning, fixing its gaze on him.

Running blindly, he had eventually hidden in a long narrow ravine, amongst the rusting remains of old cars dumped long ago. He had crossed an orderly field of pecan trees and then fled along a cow path through thick brush to come out in sight of the white shale ranch road. He didn't know what section of the road he was looking at. It was likely the section well past the creek. If he was correct, following the road to the left would take him back to the others.

Kevin moved carefully up to the fence bordering the road. His back ached from running with the weight of the Remington in his hands. He put one hand on the middle wire and, forcing it down, stepped through. His left leg caught for a moment. Laying the gun carefully down before him, he used his free hand to unhook his pants leg. He stepped on to the grassy siding of the white shale road and hastily picked up the gun.

The road stretched out featureless in both directions. Kevin crossed to the other side. He stopped and took another look down the road. It glowed luminous white in the moonlight, shaded only in a few spots by overhanging trees that appeared as dark smudges in the distance. To his right, a quarter of a mile away, he saw what might have been a curve where the road turned. But it was too distant and too dim to be sure. He looked left then right again. A pale figure was standing in middle of the road about thirty yards away.

Kevin dashed for the fence. He tossed the shotgun through into the grass beyond and using two hands, forced the middle wire down hard. Glancing over his shoulder, Kevin saw that the figure was now standing in the center of the road directly behind him. He rolled through the fence, falling. He grabbed the shotgun, righted himself, and struggling to find the safety with his fingertip, flicked it off and brought the barrel up.

Before him was the figure of a woman with her back to him. Her hair and skin were white in the moonlight. The image of her wavered and shifted. She stood with one hand rhythmically clenching and unclenching. In the other hand she held a long knife. She turned. Kevin saw her face. She looked at him with contempt and then, pointed her finger down the road to his right. With terrifying speed, she shrank back down the road from where she had come and was gone.

Chapter 8: Two Down

Warren and Sam had fallen completely silent. Warren lay on his back in the shadows. The silence around them took on a permanence that made the thought of breaking it unnerving. Their hopes were now pinned on remaining silent and invisible. James had not moved in a long while. His breathing remained shallow.

Sam heard faint sounds. Footsteps close by, and whispering. The sounds were so faint that he could not be sure if they were real or imagined. Through the small patches of moonlight, Sam saw little drifts of ground fog. As he listened intently in the silence, he realized that the usual drone of crickets was absent. Nearby, he distinctly heard footsteps, only three or so, and then silence as if they had come from nowhere and gone nowhere. He peered across at Warren, whose face was hidden in the curve of his arm.

James moved sluggishly and moaned. Relieved, Sam crawled over to where the injured boy lay and peered down. In the deep shadow, Sam could not see James' face. He continued to hover over the boy for a few more seconds then with some disappointment he prepared to draw away.

"Warren?" James said.

"No, it's Sam. Warren's over there," Sam said. He

drew his legs up under himself and sat next to James.

"I'm cold Sam. I'm real cold," James said.

"But it's hot, Jimmy" Sam said.

"I dreamed about him, Sam," James whispered.

Sam had no idea what James meant. "It's okay," he said. "We'll get out of here soon."

"They're close now," James said.

"That's good," Sam said.

"That's not who I mean..." James said.

"Just lie still," Sam said. He wanted to move back to where Warren was. Something about the way James was talking was deeply alarming. James took a long shuddering breath and spoke again.

"I saw him die," James said. "In my dream, I saw him die,"

James' hand found Sam's in the darkness. Sam's first response was to pull away. James' hand was sweaty and chilled, weak in his grasp. Sam realized James was frightened. He took hold of his hand.

"Mr. Wilson will be here any minute," Sam said.

James groaned. "They tied the man's hands up at the Hanging Tree. Then he was on a horse. He was talking so fast. They put the noose around his neck, and then the horse, it ran right out from under him, just leaving him there, kicking."

James pulled at Sam's hand.

"It didn't kill him fast. He just kept kicking. Trying to get loose. Then the rope broke, and he fell. They put him back on the horse and did it again. That time, he didn't last long. They just left him there."

Sam peered down into the darkness, trying to make out James' features in the shadows.

"Days passed by, months, I was just there watching. Then, he was back again, hanging under the tree," James said. "I think that's why McCollough set fire to it."

Sam peered about him into the dark woods. He held James' hand, feeling trapped. Sam imagined a little of what losing his own mother might be like. All he could imagine was feeling hollow. He heard someone approaching along the path. He laid James' hand on his chest, scooted quietly over to Warren, and shook him.

Warren still had his pistol in one hand. He gripped Sam's arm, peering at him in the shadows. The steps began to pass by about twenty feet off. Sam was uncertain of what to do. He gathered his courage and whispered, "Kevin!" He looked at Warren who was silent. The footsteps halted. He had barely the courage, but he whispered once more, "Kevin?"

Kevin entered the small clearing and sat heavily on the ground. They knew now that he had not made it to the house. The larger boy didn't speak. The long shotgun glinted dimly on the ground beside him. They gave him time, unwilling to break the silence.

"We didn't make it," Kevin finally said.

"How far did you get?" Warren whispered as they moved closer to the Kevin.

"It's after us," Kevin's voice had lost all its usual confidence. He stared down. He drew a long breath.

"Where's Mike?" Sam asked.

"He didn't make it," Kevin replied. They waited but Kevin said nothing more.

"What do you mean he didn't make it?" Warren asked.

"He's too slow," Kevin hissed. Suddenly his voice was raw with anger. "We didn't make it anywhere near the house. It's blocking the way. I lost Mike. Then it came after me." He took out a cigarette and lit it, his hand shaking uncontrollably.

"The Hanged Man, it got Mike?" Sam asked.

"He's up by the old barn," Kevin replied, his face lit by the glow of the cigarette tip as he inhaled.

"He's just laying up there?" Warren asked, growing more alarmed.

"Yeah, I guess so," Kevin answered.

"That's two of us down," Warren said.

James sat on a horse in the shade. Above him, the immense green form of the Hanging Tree stood motionless in the oppressive heat of the day. The sun overhead was blindingly bright. Cicadas droned in the trees. Big brown and green grasshoppers buzzed and rattled as they took flight across the fields about him.

Someone took the hat from atop his head. James' breath was rasping. He felt a burning pain in his side, but the sensation was distant, hardly worth worrying about. He shook the hair out of his eyes. He lifted his hands but found them bound and tied in front of him to his belt. He noticed two men who stood at some distance to his right, by the old dirt highway. They appeared to be brothers, each with full black beards. One wore a rose in his lapel. No, it was a red wound just above his heart. *They're dead,* James thought, and paid them no more attention.

James felt the horse beneath him shift its stance nervously, anxious to be away. Time was moving in jumps and starts. As if it was broken in brittle pieces to be picked up at random. He felt the slight weight of the rope dangling along his shoulder.

I've seen this already, James thought.

He heard a loud crack, a hand against the flank of the horse. He felt a light dizziness. No pressure on his neck at all. James sat on a horse in the shade. Above him, the immense green form of the Hanging Tree stood motionless in the oppressive heat of the day. The sun hung overhead blindingly bright. Cicadas sang loudly in the trees…

No, James thought. He halted the random play of events scattering and reforming around the Hanging Tree. It was like peering into a kaleidoscope. His brow furrowed slightly. The sky darkened and grew threatening. Something shattered and ruined, lumbered out from behind the great tree. It was a white dog.

James opened his eyes. He was lying on his back in the darkened woods. He felt a hot ache in his leg and a pounding headache behind his eyes. His mouth was dry and sour. He raised his hand and touched the thick scab that had formed above his left eye. He remembered the white light that had flashed brutally when he struck the tree. He shifted and the pain intensified.

He thought he had heard voices as he came to, but the grove was silent. He struggled to raise himself up on one elbow. Slowly, things came into focus. Mist was rising about the base of the trees. A chill crept along the ground, moving across the leaves and low shrubs, drifting over his hands and legs.

Across the way he saw three forms. It was Kevin, Sam, and Warren. They were unmoving shapes against a background of shadow and underbrush. They sat leaning in towards each other.

James was about to call out to them when he heard footsteps marching toward him through the woods. He caught the glint of dim cold light. Mist surged into the clearing, obscuring the three other boys. The leaves parted and James saw his mother.

She wore the white dress she was buried in. Her dark hair hung arranged in brittle curls. *She never wore her hair like that,* he thought. For a time, she ignored the boy, her eyes peered sharply to one side. She was listening in the silence. The whites of her eyes gleamed, reflecting the moon. Her mouth was turned down, tense.

She turned and stared directly at James. James could see her jaw flexing rhythmically as she ground her teeth. He saw her free hand, clenching and unclenching. In her other hand, she held a long silver kitchen knife. It gleamed coldly. He could see the tiny fine hairs that grew along her jaw line. He could see the taut flesh around her eyes. He could smell her, the familiar odor of talcum powder and something else, formaldehyde. She took a step forward and her face was lost in shadow.

James glanced at the vague inert forms of his friends. He painfully dragged himself backwards, retreating until he felt the firm trunk of a large tree against his back. The apparition moved to his left and crouched at the base of a second tree just a few feet away. For a moment she studied the base of the tree. Then, she rushed forward, bringing her face into the moonlight, just half a foot from James, the mask of her features now flat and emotionless. James felt a harsh chill waft across the front of his body. He drew back against the tree, pressing the back of his head against the rough bark.

She looked down again. A pale hand rose into the patch of moonlight. Her fingertips were stained with clumps of darkened blood. It was blood Warren had spit out while drawing the venom from James' leg. His own blood mixed with venom. She looked up, her features now alive with cold rage.

Uttering a stream of angry invectives James' mother brought her lips to within inches of his face. No sound emerged as she cursed him. The silent stream of words poured out from her animated face. Then she stopped, and her features became again still and dead.

She reached down toward his leg, bringing her fingers

within inches of James' snakebite. The bandage was gone. Her lips pulled back as she studied the bruised flesh. The angle of moonlight shifted like a spotlight, illuminating the pale punctures. James stared horrified as she lowered her lips to the wound.

She looked up. She was smiling. The smile became a wicked leer. Tears exploded in glistening torrents down her face as she leaned in to place ice-cold lips against James' cheek. Her face was hidden next to her son's, her familiar odor overwhelmingly strong. She began to whisper to him.

"I'm telling you, you can't make him walk out, it'll spread the venom. We've got to bring help," Warren whispered. "Somebody stays here while we get help," he said firmly.

"Kevin. Warren," Sam murmured. He grabbed each boy's arm and pointed.

They turned and looked toward where James lay in the darkness. A blurred foggy figure was bent over him. Patches of moonlight illuminated a woman's back. The woman stood and was gone.

"It's her," Kevin whispered.

James cried out, sitting bolt upright. His mouth hung open. His eyes were wide, showing whites all the way around. He stuttered, spitting and coughing. The boys were staring at him. Sam rose, uncertain of whether to approach.

Finally, James took a clear breath and spoke, the words coming haltingly.

"We have to burn the Hanging Tree," he took a long, ragged breath. "Or we won't ever get home." He convulsed and vomited a hot semicircle across the dirt beside him. Then he collapsed awkwardly, folding his arm under him. Sam moved haltingly toward him and then, gathering his courage, went to him and pulled him away from the vomit.

"We'll end up crazy as him, if we don't get out of here," Kevin said, averting his eyes.

"The creek's flooding we sure can't go that way," Warren said. Abruptly, a voice cried out in the distance. Within moments, it rose again, a high-pitched wailing.

Warren jumped up. "That's Mike," he said. The three boys hurried to the edge of the tree line. Mike stood about fifty yards away out in the open. He was calling Kevin's name between long lunging sobs.

Kevin started forward and Warren held him back. Silently, Warren pointed to a dozen or more low dark shapes, visible in the moonlight, making their way across the field.

"He's too scared to move," Warren whispered.

"He's looking for us," Sam said, cringing at the sound of Mike's wailing.

"Shine the light at him," Kevin said.

"Okay, okay," Warren said, slowly lifting the flashlight above his head. He turned it on and pointed the beam out across the field. Mike turned and the crying stopped. There was a moment of silence.

"C'mon, Mike! C'mon!" Kevin yelled and Mike was running toward them across the field. He fell once, rose, and ran on. From across the field behind him there rose coughing and growling.

"They're coming," Kevin said, raising the shotgun. Warren drew his pistol and turned the flashlight on again, wagging it side to side above his head.

"Run!" Kevin yelled. Mike staggered toward them. Behind him, the field was alive with dark low shapes crashing and stumbling through the underbrush. Mike reached the boys and fell to the ground, gasping. He stayed down on all fours struggling to regain his breath. Warren switched off the flashlight and pushed it back into his belt.

Sam opened the .410 and, fingering the one slender shotgun shell, returned it to the chamber and cocked the trigger.

Abruptly, the sounds stopped. Barely twenty yards away the vague shifting bulks drew up and halted in the grass.

The dark forms then wheeled left and charged away, moving parallel to the line of trees. The noise of their progress faded quickly with only a few stragglers moving off into the distance. The field was quiet. The boys shakily lowered their weapons. They helped Mike to his feet and pulled back into the trees.

When they returned to the clearing, Sam glanced about. "Jimmy's gone."

Chapter 9: Momma

James walked quickly through the darkened woods, his face pale and expressionless, his eyes blank. He moved decisively away from the other boys, making his way along the path by the creek, deftly side-stepping the trees that flowed by, receding behind him into the darkness. The boy's movements were stiff, a puppet being propelled by invisible strings.

"Now what?" Kevin said, the growing confusion making him angry.

Mike stared silently at Kevin in the gloom. The smaller boy was covered in scratches and cuts. His clothes were torn and muddy. A large purple bruise had formed above his eye. Dried blood trailed down the side of his head.

"You're just a damn chicken, Kevin," the smaller boy said.

"Piss off," Kevin replied vehemently.

"All your big talk, but when it comes down to it," Mike said speaking in a flat measured tone.

"You ran into the water pump," Kevin replied. "What? Am I supposed to carry you around all night whenever you decide the knock yourself out?"

"He took off and ditched me," Mike said to the others.

Kevin stepped up to Mike, towering over him.

"Look at the big man," the smaller boy said, his tone remaining flat.

"If it wasn't for you and Jimmy, we'd all be home by now. Your slow ass got you caught. Am I supposed to stay and get killed because you run like a damn girl?"

The boys were silent, digesting Kevin's explanation.

"We have to decide what to do," Warren said.

"We could just scatter. He can't follow all of us," Kevin said.

"Those things after Mike? I think they were McCollough's dogs," Warren replied.

"McCollough's dogs are dead," Mike said.

"Oh, great, what are we saying, now?" Kevin said, turning back to Mike.

"I'm saying they stink like rotting meat," Mike replied.

The boys looked at each other for a moment.

"There must be thirty of them," Warren said.

"Oh, well, that's just great," Kevin said.

"So, you ditching us all won't really help you, will it?" Mike finished.

"We don't look for Jimmy?" Sam asked quietly.

"We gotta go get your dad, Warren," Kevin said. "We gotta get out of here."

"We should look for Jimmy," Sam muttered.

"Look, we go get my dad and we come back and find Jimmy. That's if he's not already at the house...." Warren said. "He knows to do that," he concluded.

"We cross the highway?" Mike said.

"Yeah, the highway," Warren replied.

"Now that's what I'm talking about," Mike said.

The boys followed Warren out of the clearing. Sam

paused and looked back through the trees for any sign of James. The woods were still and silent. Finding himself alone, he turned and ran after the others.

James had been dreaming of walking in the sunny woods, a clear blue sky peeking down through the trees above him. Now he found himself at the edge of the tree line looking out across the nighttime fields with no idea of how he got there. His head throbbed fiercely. He could feel a painful pulse in the wound on his leg.

A little way away, he saw the white shale ranch road they had walked down earlier in the day. Pale lights flickered along the edge of his vision. Suddenly, James was awash in voices. The volume and number swelled alarmingly. His ability to concentrate was swamped by the dizzying chatter. The voices flowed forth from across the field, from the empty air about him. It was as if he had lifted the receiver of a phone to hear a hundred calls at once, each speaking insistently, oblivious to the others. The voices faded in and out, talking of crops and births and famine and deaths. Fragments of stories blended and overlapped, one into the next.

Vague shapes began to form between James and the road. Pale men and women emerged in the moonlight, walking, expressionless back and forth before him. Half aware; lives grown cold, scattered across the darkness by thousands of intervening nights. They walked, oblivious of each other, of the absence of streets or pavement or homes. Some were unaware even of the ground itself, drifting into the hard packed earth and disappearing without alarm or surprise.

Their numbers grew. They looked like they were from old photos from decades ago, or longer. They flowed past James into the darkness of the woods. Others marched away toward the road. They passed by him, oblivious to his presence, none stirring to even glance his way. The fields grew ever more crowded. James realized that they were, however listlessly, drawing closer. Circling aimlessly, but not entirely. Coming and going about him, as if drawn not by him so much as by his general location. A breeze rose in the field. The figures before him wavered and were gone, leaving it silent and empty.

James hurried out across the field. With each passing moment, he became more alert, awakening from his stupor, and in awakening, was unnerved to find himself alone again. He reached the fence and stepped through it onto the empty moonlit road. To his left, the road disappeared in the direction of the creek from where he had come. It was in that direction that he saw movement. Low shapes, dark smears coming towards him along the whiteness of the road.

James began running in the opposite direction, now fully awake, his heart hammering in his chest, agony coursing through his leg. As he ran, the familiar crawling sensation erupted along the back of his neck, his hairs standing on end as if electrified. His lungs were burning, the diluted venom in his body making him dizzy and weak.

Suddenly, a dozen yards ahead, a dog crashed against the barbed wire fence on the right. Stumbling in the dim light, it fell onto the luminous road, raising a cloud of chalky dust. James stopped. All through the fields on his right, he heard coughing and snarling.

The dog rose to its feet and, stumbling again, took up a position blocking the road. James saw more clearly as he drew closer. The animal's head hung limp from its powerful shoulders. Its neck had been broken. Clumps of dirt hung in its once white coat, suggesting that it had been buried. The burial had not lasted.

The beast struggled to raise its head, shambling

forward a few feet. In the spill of moonlight, James saw a slow writhing along the animal's shoulders and back, as if the muscles were quivering and flowing beneath its matted white fur. The dog was not white. It was covered in a dense layer of pale maggots. More dogs were emerging in the moonlight, approaching from the field on his right. James ran forward seeking to get past to one side. The dog turned its head on its broken neck, rolled one eye up toward him and lunged.

James aimed a violent kick at the animal's head, the power of the blow sending a shock wave up his leg. He felt the beast's head give way against the crown of his foot. It tore loose from the dog's body, a spray of maggots spilling across the ground. The headless body struggled to right itself. James dodged past it and ran. More of the animals crossed the fence line onto the road behind him. He raced on, the luminous white road hurtling by beneath his feet.

His lungs were burning as he came to a long aluminum gate on his left. He leapt up on it and threw himself over, landing on the cattle guard that spanned the space beyond. Rising, he pelted off down the dirt ranch road that led away from the gate. Behind him, he heard the dogs as they crashed through the fence line in pursuit.

He ran on. Ahead, the windmill glinted above the trees along the curve of the road. Faltering and exhausted, James glanced over this shoulder back along the road. He stopped. There was no longer any movement. The road was empty. James realized he was terribly thirsty. He hurried painfully down the road toward the cistern he and the boys had visited that afternoon. He came to a gate. But it was not a cattle gate. The little gate, held closed by a simple latch, was part of a low wooden fence painted white. James let himself into the yard and looked up to see a house before him.

What he had expected to be the new feed barn was now a single-story farmhouse with a stacked stone chimney. To one side, the windmill still stood. Beneath it, the low circular cistern they had visited earlier that day. Around him, the yard was empty, save for a few pieces of archaic farm equipment. The old windows of the house were dark, the panes of glass blurring the reflection of the moonlit yard like ripples in water.

James went to the cistern and drank deeply. Rain began to fall lightly in the yard. James looked up, puzzled by the drifting mist of rain. Hadn't the sky just been clear? Lightning flickered, illuminating from within the forms of clouds now rising to obscure the stars. Lighting erupted followed by a deafening roll of thunder. James turned toward the house as the rain began to fall heavily. He approached it warily, stepping gingerly up onto the porch. The boards were old and gray. They creaked but held. He walked down the length of the porch to the door, which was framed on either side by tall windows.

James put his hand on the doorknob. *This is from my dream,* he thought. The doorknob rattled loosely as he turned it. The door swung inward. Lightning flashed, throwing a long pillar of white light across the floor before him, outlining his elongated shadow. James saw that a second room beyond the first, half visible through a wide doorway, was lit from the side by perhaps a single candle, out of his line of sight. It threw a warm flickering light across the floor and against the blank walls. Beyond that room James could see another interior doorway and blackness. The lightning flashed again.

James stepped into the darkened front room as a wall of water struck the roof and cascaded off the windows. He walked gingerly. Setting his feet one in front of the other, testing the old floorboards, he made his way toward the second room. Lightning flashed. He glanced to his right and saw a window that looked out onto the front yard. He turned toward it, away from the faint glow of the second room. On the wall near him, hung small, framed photographs. As the lightning flashed, he saw they were tintypes, blank faces staring into the camera.

The temperature dropped rapidly as he stood peering out onto the yard. His breath was visible before him. Thunder rocked the house. He heard glass shatter in a distant room. Something had fallen to the floor. A blast of lightning lit the yard for long seconds. Across the way, stood the windmill and the cistern. The rain fell in heavy sheets partly obscuring the yard. The roar of rain falling against the tin roof was deafening.

James remained at the window. For long moments the yard was dark. Thunder rolled in the distance but no longer reached its peak. James placed his hand against the glass and rubbed the fog from the windowpane. He peered out, looking in vain for any detail in the gloom of the yard. The glass was cold.

The lightning came again, and light spilled across the yard. Beneath the windmill he saw a woman. She stood facing him, her arms at her side. Something glinted in her hand. The lightning winked out. James heard a sound from the room behind him.

He turned stepping away from the window. There, in the pool of warm light on the floorboards beyond the interior doorway, a blurred shadow rocked, undulating. Misshapen, it swayed back and forth. James felt a strange anticipation rising in him. He stepped forward, drawn by the sinuous shadowy motions. It was a vaguely human shape.

The shadow form of the figure was elongated, its head, disproportioned. Judging from its movements, it seemed to be something that, unlike the spirits roaming the open fields, was very much awake and aware, a different thing entirely. Its shadow capered in a slow and lithesome dance on the creaking floorboards of the darkened house.

The rain slowed some, quieting its frantic drumbeat on the tin roof. James took another tenuous step forward. The shadow abruptly withdrew and disappeared, leaving an empty shaft of warm light beyond the doorway. James took a step back. The shadow rose again into the light, moving with the same sinuous rhythm, arms circling about its hips and its head. James stepped into the doorway.

No figure confronted him. Before him against one wall was a long table. On it, was a single candle, burning low. Already it sputtered and flickered in the cross currents that moved through the house. Next to the candle, its head cocked at an angle, there sat a red cardinal. It stood on the table examining him. Its black eyes shone brightly. Its plumage was blood red in the warm light of the candle's small flame. It leapt off the table, took wing, and swept from the room, leaving by the darkened doorway opposite, disappearing toward the back of the house.

There was a crash against the front door. Spinning, James saw the door swing wide. A flash of lightning illuminated the form of the Hanged Man as it lurched into the front room. The candle on the table hissed and sputtered out, plunging the house into darkness.

James rushed through into the third room at the back of the house. He crashed into a wall and began to grope for a way out. Something fluttered against his face in the darkness. He raised his hands to ward it off and felt the dense cold body of the Hanged Man before him. James thrashed wildly backwards, careening off a wall. He felt a brittle hand clawing at his arm and shoulder. A stifling chill rolled across him.

"No!" he screamed. He fought with all his strength to

evade the hard hands that scraped his face and clutched at his arms. Lightning flashed, pouring light in through a doorway leading outside.

Before him, lit for an instant, the Hanged Man blotted out the world, its face above him, rigid and expressionless. James dropped towards the floor and scrambled, feeling himself half lifted by his shirt before it tore loudly, and the floor rushed up to meet him again. James scrambled for the open doorway, lit blue in a flash of blowing rain. His hand settled on something cold. Before him, in another flash of light, he saw it, the face of a woman. She sat upright against the wall, blonde hair spilling down her front past a splash of crimson, her eyes wide and staring inches in front of his face. James scrambled back and away across the floor. Again, the lightning flashed. He turned to see that the Hanged Man had stopped in the center of the room. James crawled madly along the wall towards the doorway.

Thunder crashed, deafening. Above even the roar of the thunder, James heard and felt a series of violent concussions. Plaster rained down on him. He heard another violent collision and felt a shudder go through the floorboards beneath him. Lightning stuttered across the sky outside, remaining impossibly long. He saw the woman, upright against the far wall; dressed in a high collared gown, torn down to expose an ugly red wound. Her long blonde hair was dizzyingly bright in the flash of lightning that lingered. Her hands lay open, palms up, on the floor. Across her lap, lay a rifle. She stared ahead, oblivious.

The Hanged Man threw himself rebounding from wall to wall above the pale figure on the floor. Clouds of plaster fell where it drove deep gouging holes in the walls. James saw its dead expression rotate wildly past, as the Hanged Man careened away inches above him. James made it to the open doorway and out into the rain.

He fell off the back porch onto the wet ground. The rain slacked off, dropping to a drizzle. James turned to look back towards the house. Inside, the violent concussions had ended. He turned, glancing about the yard. The fields ran away in all directions. He turned back toward the house. On the porch, drifting gently side to side was the Hanged Man. It dropped slowly off the porch and moved toward him. Moonlight broke through the clouds illuminating the smooth curve of the cement water cistern. James bolted across the muddy yard towards the windmill. He felt a violent blow against the side of his head. He rose stunned and lunged again for the cistern, which stood less than ten feet away.

She's got a taste for the water at the well, McCollough had said. James stumbled, falling. He pushed off his right hand and kept running.

James felt cold knuckles against his back as the Hanged Man took hold of his collar. He tried desperately to duck his head out of his shirt but then the hands were on his throat, and it was too late. He thrashed about, clawing at the coldness, kicking wildly. It was like steel cable had been wrapped about his neck. The Hanged Man's fingers clamped down unbearably tight. James saw the cistern circle away out of his line of vision. He clawed at the hands, which burned with coldness. They were immovable. He could feel the front of his throat collapsing, causing him to gag, bile spilling across his tongue. Spots of light swam before his eyes. He saw the yard drifting gently by. He heard a faint grinding of his own bones in his ears. He struggled to draw a last breath. There was only the gentle rotation of the yard and the fields beyond.

You were right, Momma, it's not safe here.

James heard a dull thump. He felt it through the hands that gripped him. They dropped away and he fell heavily to the ground. His legs felt numb and useless beneath him. He crawled blindly forward, coughing, and choking. He found his hand on the edge of the cistern, which appeared out of the bright spots swimming before his eyes.

He rolled over the edge of the cistern and into the shocking cold of the water. Immediately, he found his footing and rose. The water poured off him, flowing down him as he stood. Before him, was the Hanged Man, drifting warily along the edge of the cistern, unwilling to cross over the edge.

She's got a taste for the water at the well.

James backed toward the center of the big circular tank. The Hanged Man moved closer and then drifted back, its hands twitching. James stood staring at the thing as it hung in the air before him.

The sky was again calm. The night was silent save for the sound of water dripping from James' hands, ringing as it fell back into the tank. James studied the Hanged Man's face, leathery and cracked, its lips long ago drawn back, leaving a moist wet space ringed with teeth. Its eyes saw nothing; black marbles that shone dully in their hard sockets. James sensed that it was, for all its supernatural horror, somewhat simple minded.

The Hanged Man turned to circle the tank and it was then that he saw it. Buried deep into its back, gleaming in the moonlight, was the silver blade of a long dark-handled kitchen knife. The boy began to laugh. It was an ugly barking sound, the veil of frail sanity slipping away from him. The house, with its grisly scene of death shimmered, fading. The white wooden fence became a pale fog, drifting away. A breeze rose. The feed barn, real and in the present, flickered into focus. Tall posts and barbed wire surrounded the yard. Above James, the blades of the windmill began to turn. Clear water tumbled into the tank from the pipe that looped over its edge.

Still laughing, James dunked both hands down and threw a hand full of water up and out towards the Hanged Man. It slapped across its chest, squealing like ice on a hot stove. James splashed up more. An explosion of steam and hot fumes erupted as the Hanged Man raced away across the yard to disappear like storm-tossed paper down the long dark dirt road.

James raised his hands, capering in the thigh deep water, screaming, "Mama!" He kept screaming until his voice failed him.

Chapter 10: A Free Ride

The four boys stood at the edge of the trees having a fierce but muted debate. Beyond them, stretched an open field, crossed by two fence lines. Past that, was the Interstate. Every few minutes, a truck, traveling late into the evening swept past to disappear toward the big green interstate signs that glowed in the distance.

"I don't give a damn if there's fifty of them, they're just dogs," Kevin said. He was staring down at Mike.

"They're not just dogs," Mike answered in a harsh whisper. He turned and glanced toward the nearest fence between them and the highway. Low figures moved about in the dim moonlight. He turned to Warren and Sam who leaned in, listening to the argument. "They're not dogs anymore," he pleaded.

"I'm going," Kevin said.

Mike grabbed his arm.

Kevin stepped past Mike, brushing him aside. "Okay, then, so we vote," he said brightly. "Who's going that way to the highway right now? He pointed and raised his hand.

Sam exhaled loudly and raised his.

Warren looked at Mike. "Mike, we're going," he said.

In the distance, the field was flat and gray, marked in places by deeper low spots and shadows. Beyond the black fence posts they saw shapes moving about.

Warren turned to Kevin. He pointed to a bright highway sign glowing in the distance. "There's a storm drain past the first fence. It runs all the way under the highway. We can take it the rest of the way."

Three of the boys began walking. Mike stood still. In moments, the others were twenty paces away and growing more distant. Finally, he bolted after them. They all walked quickly across the open ground, staying close together, reaching the first fence line without incident. Whatever the dogs were doing, they remained at a distance.

Kevin held open the barbed wires of the fence as the other boys stepped through. He climbed through last. Warren scaled a fence post and stood like an acrobat on the wobbling middle wire, straddling the post.

"There it is," Warren said. He was pointing toward a big shadow in the field that marked the entrance to the storm drain. He dropped to the ground and the four continued on, arriving at the entrance of the drain. It was fed by a low sloping gully. The entrance to the drain was dry but utterly black.

"Not going in there," Kevin said.

"Me, neither," Sam said.

"Yeah, okay," Warren responded.

The boys moved on past the drain. About thirty yards away, a shotgun blast boomed. The blinding muzzle flash hung for a moment against the backdrop of glowing highway signs before them.

"Jesus Christ!" Mike yelled as heavy shotgun pellets smacked his chest and face. Raising his hand, he felt the small tears on his forehead where the pellets had split the skin. A haggard figure could be seen in the distance lurching towards them. Mike bolted back the way they had come, racing for the protection of the gully, tumbling into the shadows as a second blast echoed. He scurried into the pitch-blackness of the drain, followed closely by the others.

"What the hell?" Sam yelled. "I'm bleeding!" The boys hurried down the drain tunnel, jammed close together in the darkness, shuffling along with their heads slightly down.

"We need light!" Mike screamed as he slowed down in the absolute darkness. His high-pitched voice echoed up and down the pipe. All four boys were jammed together, with Mike in front who would not go forward without light and by Sam at the end who fought to push past them. Warren and Kevin began to lose control to the collective rising panic and claustrophobia. An elbow struck Sam in the face, knocking the back of his head against the cement tunnel. Stars exploded across his vision. He fell forward grabbing on to someone.

Warren stumbled and slid down the rough curve of the tunnel struggling to pull out his flashlight, which was trapped beneath him. He shoved hard with his foot at the figure before him not certain of who or what it was. Beneath him, the hard form of a rifle was jammed against his side, blocking him from reaching the flashlight. Out of the darkness came a violent blow. Warren felt his nose give. Blood poured out. He kicked viciously. Mike was screaming over and over the same thing. Warren felt a second body fall against him. The screaming was now right in his ear.

"Stop fighting, stop fighting!" Mike yelled. "STOP FIGHTING!"

Finally, the meaning of the words sank in. Warren covered his face and balled himself up, holding still.

Kevin fell back against the wall of the tunnel. The boys were a tangle of limbs. Sam felt a shotgun pellet rub loose from the skin of his cheek and fall into his hand. The sound of heavy breathing was echoing up and down the pipe. Warren finally turned on the flashlight, swinging it first one way and then the other down the tunnel, illuminating the grassy slope at the near end and the long smooth expanse of tunnel before them as it faded into the distance.

Kevin raised himself and found his shotgun where it was wedged beneath Warren. He pulled the gun loose, scraping the stock along the cement.

"Get that light out of my face," he said.

Blood was running in a long smear down Kevin's chin. His lower lip was split wide open. Warren ran his sleeve across his mouth. It came back deep red.

Kevin reached down and helped Mike to his feet.

"Okay. We're not fighting anymore," he said.

"Let's just have the two biggest guys beat the shit out of each other," Mike said angrily. He spat contemptuously.

"Quiet!" Warren said. He was shining his flashlight down the tunnel at the grassy slope where they had entered. Instantly the others were silent. The crunch of pebbles beneath boots could be heard.

"Go, go, go," Warren whispered harshly, pushing the others.

Warren continued looking toward the opening as Kevin, Mike and Sam raced away into the darkness behind him. The footsteps at the entrance of the tunnel stopped. There was a dull metallic click. Warren began backing quickly down the tunnel. Then he faced forward and ran. He turned every few moments and shone the flashlight back at the entrance to see if they were being followed. The only sound in the tunnel was the frantic scuffle of feet. Warren heard the boys moving away before him. He raised the flashlight to the top of the tunnel and shone it forward to give the rest some light before shining it back behind him again.

More than once, he banged his knuckles badly on the top of the tunnel. Sweat poured down his face as he ran along in a half crouch. He tried to accurately judge the growing distance, but the tunnel was so uniform that he had no idea how far from the entrance he was. He knew intimately what a shotgun would do at close range. He involuntarily recalled the rabbits he had burned out of brush piles and shot. The skin along his back twitched as he ran along the tunnel.

"C'mon, C'mon," he whispered. The others were now well ahead of him. Being the rear guard was slowing his progress considerably. Again, he turned and shone the flashlight back down the tunnel. There, in the distant gloom he saw the glint of metal.

"Get down!" Warren screamed as he fell forward. He flicked off the flashlight and pulled loose his pistol. The sound of the shotgun was deafening in the cement confines of the tunnel. The distant muzzle flash lit the rough cement before his face throwing long shadows from tiny pebbles that made up the surface. Pellets squealed harshly along the walls throwing dust as they ricocheted down the tunnel and on toward the other boys. Warren felt a jolt along the base of one foot.

Without rising from his prone position, Warren pointed his pistol back along the tunnel and fired two shots. The boom of the pistol was incredibly loud in the confined space, the muzzle flash nearly blinding. He rose, and sighting on the end of the tunnel, fired continuously until he heard the click of the firing pin on spent shells. He ran on, stuffing the flashlight into his pocket and then digging for shells in the pouch on his belt.

Warren ran guided by the curve of the tunnel beneath his feet. He flipped open the pistol and dumped the empty shell casings onto the tunnel floor. Then, pointing the barrel down as he stumbled along, he pushed a shell into the first of the empty chambers. He tripped and fell forward to one knee. The tunnel rang with shells falling out of his still open pouch.

"Warren!" someone yelled from ahead.

"I'm coming, don't shoot!" he yelled. Using his free hand, which was partially full of shells, he forced the snap to close on the pouch. Then, rising and running on in a low crouch, he began loading again. The harsh sound of his own breathing echoed about him. The shuffle of his boots on the cement unusually loud in his ears. His ankle felt twisted. He closed the cylinder on the pistol and felt for his flashlight.

The second blast caught him upright. He saw the muzzle flash and tried to throw himself forward. He felt a spread of pellets hit him from the base of his head down to the small of his back. He pitched forward, the gun spinning free from his hand. He rose and lunged forward in the darkness, scrambling to find where the pistol had skidded to a stop at the center of the pipe. Before him, the image of the mutilated rabbit swam against the darkness. Its eyes were wide, blinking frantically.

He found the pistol, rose, turned and fired six times, placing the rounds as carefully as he could down the center of the tunnel. Numbness began to swim slowly across his back, then searing pain. He felt tears start down his face.

"Warren!" a voice yelled from almost directly in front of him.

He ran headlong into Kevin. The two boys fell to the floor as a third round of pellets skidded past on the walls. As he fell, Warren struggled to open the cylinder of his pistol. His shoulder struck the hard cement floor. Chunks of lead hit him in his forearm and peppered Kevin across his thigh.

"Get out of the way!" Kevin yelled, shoving Warren bodily to the floor behind him. Then he rose, lifting the Remington to this shoulder.

The .20 gauge boomed three times, belching flame down the tunnel. Smoke rolled across them as Warren struggled to get new rounds into his pistol. Kevin turned the shotgun over and stuffed in the shotgun shells he had scattered on the floor before him. He searched in the dark for a third shell, found it, jammed it in, and flipped the gun back over. Warren snapped the cylinder closed on the .38.

Both boys began firing. The tunnel echoed with a deafening hail of gunfire. The muzzle flashes lit up the tunnel wall far into the distance. They emptied their guns into the choking cloud and turned to run for the end of the tunnel.

Mike and Sam had scrambled out of the storm drain and up the embankment that ran along side of the highway. Now the two of them sat together, peering at the exit of the tunnel below them. Sam kept his shotgun trained on the entrance. They heard the dull plunk of gunfire and heard the whistle of pellets exiting the storm drain.

"Jesus," Mike said as the third shotgun blast sounded. "They're getting killed." Six pistol shots sounded like they were coming from inside a metal can, ringing. Mike scooted back down to the edge.

"Don't look in, you'll get one in the eye," Sam said.

They heard Kevin yelling and then three successive shotgun blasts, much louder and closer.

Sam shouted, "They'll be coming out."

More gunfire followed. Mike and Sam could see the flashes along the edge of the drain tunnel. Then Warren and Kevin burst out of the tunnel and scrambled up the hillside. Warren was grimacing visibly as Kevin struggled to push him up towards the highway.

"He's been shot!" Kevin yelled breathless. The boys stopped at the top of the embankment. Kevin was forcing more shells into the shotgun. He flipped it back over and aimed it toward the tunnel exit. They all watched the dark hole.

"Are you hurt bad?" Kevin said, not taking his eyes off the tunnel. He wiped at his blood-stained chin.

Sam and Mike scrambled over to Warren. Sam lifted Warren's shirt. Purple bruises the size of quarters were forming across his back. Sam brushed two pellets out of shallow wounds with the flat of his hand.

"God dammit!" Warren pulled violently away. He was crying. He sat heavily and began to fumble with his pistol. His hands were shaking so much that he had trouble getting shells into the cylinders. The wounds on his back were stiffening. He laid the pistol in his lap and gripped his upper thighs with his rigid hands.

"God, it hurts," he murmured, trembling as waves of pain washed over him.

"I'm gonna flag down a car," Sam said. He handed the .410 shotgun to Mike, took the flashlight from Warren and scrambled out onto the road.

The interstate disappeared in either direction. The full moon hung like a lantern over the trees in the direction of Luling. It was dropping toward the horizon now and would soon be gone. Sam was jumpy. He kept glancing back down toward the others on the embankment, afraid that at any second something would emerge from the tunnel.

Suddenly, he saw a pair of headlights.

"Someone's coming, I see em!" he yelled.

The other boys started up the slope. Sam signaled with the flashlight at the oncoming car. The other boys crouched along the shoulder of the road. Sam waved the flashlight.

He stepped a few feet out onto the road and waved it some more.

Mike peered down the highway to his left. In the distance, the car seemed to be weaving a little. One headlight was not aligned. It was weak and yellow. Mike heard gears grinding as the car drew closer and changed lanes into the nearest one. Mike glanced back at the tunnel. Kevin continued to watch it, looking up only occasionally to check the progress of the car. Sam inched out a little further into the road. He continued to wave the flashlight in broad sweeping arcs. Something seemed wrong. The car disappeared behind a rise and then appeared again rising over the last hill. It entered a flat stretch, now just half a mile away, without slowing.

"Something's wrong!" Mike yelled. "Sam! Where did the interstate signs go?"

The highway was dark. The signs they had seen illuminating the Luling exits were no longer there. They had simply vanished. Sam stepped away from the road, lowering his flashlight. They heard the howl of tires along with the hammering of metal on metal as a big black sedan swept past and shuddered to a halt a few feet up the road.

The boys stared at the car. It was old. The front end was badly damaged. One wheel rattled as the driver ground the transmission into reverse and the big car lumbered backwards to halt before them. The hood was covered in mud and algae. The front windshield was badly damaged. Smoke poured out from under the buckled hood. The driver side window nearest them was a mosaic of cracked glass glinting in the moonlight. Slowly, Sam turned the flashlight on the window. It shone with a deep red stain.

A pale face pushed up against the window from within. A chin and teeth were momentarily outlined, the jaw flapping frantically before the face drew back into the red darkness. The car idled roughly, a pinging sound coming from the transmission.

The window was lowered a few inches. Water ran from beneath the car. "You boys look wore out!" said a voice from inside the car.

A second car appeared over the hill, this time coming from the opposite direction. It was on fire, burning as it shuddered down the road. Long yellow tongues of flame rolled off it into the night sky. About half a mile away, it swerved left and cut across the grassy lane divider. It rumbled up onto the nearest lane, coming the wrong way down the highway.

"Boys!" the voice yelled from the big black car before them, "Better let me take you down the road!" The back door nearest them swung open, howling on its old hinges. A wall of water poured out onto the highway, trickling away into a dribble as the car emptied out. Inside it was utterly black.

"Boys!" the driver said. "I know you got lots of fine plans for yerselves, getting' cars and workin' a job and taking off some little gal's panties and all that, but don't make this hard on yerselves."

The four boys began to back down the embankment toward the tunnel. Sam stepped to the edge of the tunnel shining the flashlight in.

"It's empty!" he yelled.

Mike, his eyes wide with fear pushed past him. "Screw this!" he yelled as he plunged back into the tunnel. Warren followed him in. The second car, burning fiercely, slammed into the first, knocking it backwards. Flames poured out of the driver side window of the new arrival.

"C'mon in boys," a second voice bellowed. "It's air conditioned!"

Something, black and grisly stood up out of the first

car.

"We're just here to help you up the road!"

"They're coming!" Sam yelled. Kevin looked over his shoulder and saw a gaunt figure, lit from behind, lurching down the side of the embankment, its arms flapping wildly. They scrambled down into the drain tunnel, heading back into the darkness.

"He'll show you no mercy!" the voice roared, followed by another deafening crash that blotted out the light from the flames. Chunks of metal careened along the tunnel behind them.

"Let me look!" Kevin yelled. He took the flashlight from Sam, forcing his way to the front, shining the flashlight before him. Through the haze of the tunnel, they saw nothing. The boys surged forward again.

Exiting the far side, they clambered up the gully to ground level, and turned, gasping, to look back toward the highway. There were no flames. There were no cars. There was only the green glow of the flickering highway signs marking the exits to Luling along Interstate 90. A single truck making its way toward San Antonio disappeared into the distance.

"Jesus, what are we gonna do?" Mike said.

Chapter 11: Reunion

Kevin sat with the others amid the trees that ran along the creek. His leg was torn and bleeding, the wound hot and painful. He looked at the tip of the shotgun barrel. It was clumped with rotted flesh and hunks of hair. The dogs had come at them after they exited the tunnel, driving them away from the highway and back toward the creek. In the worst moments, Kevin hadn't had time to reload, and instead had used the shotgun as a club. The other boys had broken free and run.

Kevin took a handful of leaves and wrapping them around the barrel, pulled the length of it through his hand. He felt the sharp edges of bone chips as he dropped them. Maggots writhed on the leaves. Kevin saw a dozen more inching along the caked barrel. He wiped the stock and barrel again and moved away from the maggots squirming on the ground.

Warren sat, leaning slightly forward, his shoulders hunched; shivers of pain running through him. Mike and Sam were focused on Kevin.

The larger boy seemed diminished, his eyes down, his expression clouded and uncertain. He ran his fingertips across the wound on his leg. The shotgun pellets had raised ugly bruises beneath the thick material of his blue jeans. A dull ache was setting in, making running painful, and he was getting tired. He knew he was slowing down.

"What the hell is happening?" Kevin said.

The boys looked at him with increasing worry.

"What is happening?" Kevin repeated. He lifted the bloody shirt away from his body, as if noticing it for the first time. Warren groaned loudly. He pushed forward onto his knees and laying his forearms along the ground, put his head down on the cool earth.

"What do we do?" Mike asked.

"Why do you do that?" Kevin replied.

"What do you mean?" Mike said.

"I mean, how should I know?" Kevin replied, the edge of anger in his voice growing. "Why am I supposed to decide all the time?"

Warren had raised his head. He looked at Kevin, frowning.

"Because…," Mike said, the pitch of his voice rising.

"You always do this…," Kevin said. "I mean, why am I always the…." His words trailed off.

There was a long pause. Then Kevin was crying. Warren sat upright. He and the other boys' eyes were wide. As Kevin wept, his hands, full veined and strong, lay inert; curled gently atop the stock of the shotgun across his lap. He finally said, "I don't want to die like that," gesturing vaguely out toward the field. His tears spilled down his face.

"We're not gonna die," Sam said, growing increasingly frightened.

"People die all the time," Kevin answered. "Just like that." He snapped his fingers.

"Kevin don't be…," Sam pleaded.

"Oh, I see what you want. You want me to act like we're all gonna be okay," Kevin replied, slowly nodding yes. "I see, I see." He wiped his nose with the back of his hand. "Well, how about this. My mother died just driving us to church. One minute, she's lecturing me. Then the door on her side comes halfway past the steering wheel. The car horn is blowing. I'm up under the dash. She's just looked at me. There was all this blood, my hands kept slipping."

Kevin lowered his head. "It was my…" he whispered. He took a deep ragged breath. The boys looked at each other. Kevin raised his head, his face contorted.

"I undid my seatbelt, and she was telling me to put it back on," Kevin said. "But I wasn't gonna do it. So, she starts trying to get the belt on me and drive at the same time." Kevin looked at them waiting for some reaction. Exasperated, he added, "She ran a light."

The magnitude of what he was saying settled on the boys. Mike shook it off, first.

"It's not your fault," Mike said.

"Why do you *do* that? It was exactly my fault. Stop looking at me all the time like I'm supposed to know *anything,*" Kevin pleaded.

"You were only a little kid," Sam said quietly.

Kevin was shaking his head *no,* his hand pressed hard against his lips. Then, he lost himself to it. He sobbed, head down, his body shaking and heaving. The boys waited. There was nothing else to do.

Eventually, Kevin's crying slowed and came to a halt. He took a deep breath. He gathered himself and slowly stood, turning away from them, pushing his hair back. He shook out his arms, letting the weight of the shotgun dangle and took a deep breath. He fished out his pack of cigarettes and searched through it. They were all bent. He took one, straightened it, and finding a match, lit it. He took a deep pull of smoke and blew it out, feeling the swell of nicotine course through him. Sam stood and put out his hand about chest high. Kevin passed him the cigarette. Sam took it. They saw the taller boy's confidence return to his posture. Sam took a puff and handed him back the cigarette.

A moment passed.

"We gotta go," Warren said.

"Can you walk?" Kevin asked him.

Warren's teeth were clinched tightly. "I can do whatever."

A shotgun boomed in the distance. Pellets rattled through the leaves about them.

"Bastard's still after us," Sam said. With that, the boys were up and moving. They strode along the path following Warren's flashlight.

Another dull bang echoed from farther away. The boys fled, racing past the trees that lurched out of the darkness into the dim yellow glow of the flashlight beam. The moon, fast disappearing, offered little light in the depth of the woods.

And there he was in front of them, James, bent over, his hands on his knees. He looked up at them, out of breath. Kevin grabbed James by the arm, half in anger and half in relief. "Where the hell have you been?" he said.

"We have to burn the tree," James said. "We have to burn the Hanging Tree."

The boys looked at him, silently. He began again.

"It causes everything, him, the dogs, and everything."

Kevin dismissed him with a wave of his hand.

"We're not going back there again," Kevin said.

"We don't have a choice," James said, raising his voice.

"We can go to the barn and cross to the house. We almost made it last time," Mike said.

"You didn't almost make it!" James yelled at them. "It's just playing a game with us. That's why McCollough tried to burn it. He knew. I'm telling you; the Hanging Tree is why this is happening."

"No, Jimmy," Kevin said, waving him off.

James dropped his voice. "Stop arguing with me just to argue, Kevin! If we keep running, it'll just chase us down. It's a game and the game ends soon. Listen to me. The Hanging Tree is...is the center of everything that's happening."

"Why listen to you?" Warren said, grimacing.

"Because I'm the one here who *knows,*" James said.

Kevin got a sour look on his face. He rolled his eyes.

"You know I'm the one," James repeated, keying on Kevin.

"I know you're a freak," Kevin replied.

"I'm a lot more than a freak," James said, speaking low. "I can see em. You know I can see 'em." James was trembling. It was an admission he had never made directly to anyone.

Kevin turned away. "To hell with this," he said.

"No, Kevin. You tell them," James said, his voice rising. He grabbed Kevin's arm and turned him back. On contact, Kevin's body went rigid. James saw the image of his mother on the ranch road. It was a simple thing, like opening a book.

"What are you doing?" Kevin said, falling back on the ground. His eyes wide with fear. "What are you doing to me!" he screeched, throwing one arm up across his eyes, backing away across the dirt. James followed, bearing down on him.

"You saw her, on the road, tonight," James said, laughing harshly. "You saw my mother. She was there and you saw her. Who's the freak now, Kevin?" Kevin balked. His mouth opened as if to say something and then closed again. He began to look around at the others.

"Tell em what we're gonna do, Kevin. They always listen to you," James said. Kevin struggled to produce some kind of response, his jaw working soundlessly.

James thrust out his hand, threatening to grab the taller boy again. "You want to see more? They hung people in that tree, one after another, after another. And now it's like a battery. It draws in anybody who dies on the highway, anybody who dies in town. It's drawing them for miles around."

He turned and looked at Warren. "During the fire, Warren. We all felt it. Just before the wind came," he said emphatically.

Warren looked down at his feet, confused. "The cars on the highway," Warren finally said.

"Oh no, no, no..." Mike moaned.

"Tell em, Kevin," James repeated.

There was a pause.

"He's not lying," Kevin said. "He knows.".

"Oh, man," Mike said.

"We have to move," James said. He felt the swarming pressure growing in his head. "Warren, which way to the tree? No, forget it." He looked around over his shoulder. "I know where it is." He began to walk away.

"Wait a minute," Sam said. "This is what we're doing?"

"He'll be here in a minute," James said.

"McCollough died. We saw it," Mike said, whining.

James spun on his heel to face them again. "Don't be so blind. Of course, he's dead. Just like the dogs," James said. He turned and began walking again, the boys exchanged glances and then followed. James felt dizzy. He began to hear voices again, distant, and unclear. Abruptly, his vision went blank.

He saw the old woman, standing on the tip of a fence

post. Balanced perfectly against a field of stars, flapping her arms, her old flesh jiggling. She was laughing hysterically, yelling, waving her hands in the air. Blood welled up from her eyes and poured down her face, as if being forced out by immense pressure from within her head. The image faded.

James heard Sam next to him. He felt Sam's hand beneath his arm. James was collapsing. He regained his legs and continued walking.

"...supposed to burn the thing down?" Sam was saying.

James tried to close off his mind; to keep it a blank. *The old woman was someone to McCollough.* He felt sick.

"You've got gasoline somewhere, Warren?" James said. "Where is it?"

"There's kerosene at the old barn," Warren answered.

"You get the kerosene, Warren" James said. "We'll..." He glanced at Kevin and Sam. "We'll try and draw him away."

"How you gonna do that?" Warren asked.

James let out an ugly barking laugh. "Aw hell, Warren, they're all following me now."

"Wait." Warren said struggling with his confusion. "Just let me think." He was shivering. Sweat was running down his face and arms. A moment passed and then, making up his mind, he said, "Mike, you're going with me."

"Why me?" Mike asked, incredulous.

"Because I don't have the key to the barn, and you're small enough to go through the window," Warren answered irritably.

"Aw, man..." Mike said, but being needed by the larger boy raised an echo of pride somewhere in him. He squared his small shoulders and spit.

"Whatever happens, burn the tree," James said, and he started walking again. They walked briskly, no longer speaking. They reached the edge of the field where McCollough had died. Warren took out his pistol.

"C'mon," he said to Mike.

With that, Warren and Mike headed away across the open field towards the old white barn. Kevin and Sam watched them go for a moment and then turned and followed James who was already heading away in the opposite direction toward the Hanging Tree.

Chapter 12: Alone Again

Warren and Mike crossed the field and began jogging along the ranch road that ran up toward the old barn. Mike could hear Warren's breathing coming in gasps. The moon was low. The field was growing darker. Warren was not using his flashlight. Suddenly, he stopped.

"They're here," Warren said, gasping. A rotting smell drifted past them. From down by the creek, three muffled shotgun blasts sounded in the distance.

"Here we go," Mike whispered.

Warren turned on his flashlight. Before them were half a dozen of McCollough's dogs blocking the road, their flyblown bodies puckered with rot. The stench rolled over them.

"We're going over the top of the hill. But don't run," Warren whispered. They began backing away. Warren turned and headed into the shrubs and trees on the hillside. For the second time that night, Mike plunged into the thick tangle.

James walked parallel to the tree line. Abruptly, he stopped. A dull clicking sound began repeating over and over from within the trees. "Come out," James said.

McCollough separated from the dark foliage and took

a few halting steps into the field. His head seen in silhouette in the dim light was misshapen, stained black on one side.

"He's gonna break your little necks," McCollough gurgled. He raised the double-barreled shotgun, pointing it at them. The boys flinched. The clicking sound was McCollough cocking the hammers and pulling the trigger over and over. Kevin and Sam stepped back. James didn't.

"What do you want?" James said in a flat voice. The image of the woman with the wound in her chest that James had seen in the house came on full force. James could see every detail of her. *What's he trying to tell me?*

"It had to start somewhere," McCollough croaked. The hammers of the double barrel shotgun had stopped clicking for a moment. McCollough took a few halting steps closer. His features were slack. Only his mouth still moved, sputtering, and showing his teeth. Clumps of dirt clung to the side of his face. Part of the crown of his head was missing. This was the source of the black liquid running down the side of his head.

The image of the woman winked out. McCollough stumbled momentarily, as if his strings had been cut. He exhaled, sputtering. Then, he started toward the boys with long stiff-legged steps. "Don't you boys run from me! You been stirring things up!"

"Shoot him," James said, glancing toward Kevin. Kevin held the shotgun before him, but the barrel was slightly down. As the thing that had once been McCollough charged forward, yelling, black sticky blood blew out in small spurts from multiple bullet wounds in his chest and throat. The tiny mists of black blood trailed behind the lurching figure like steam from a locomotive. McCollough's head dangled to one side. He raised a hand to grip his hair and hold his head upright.

"He'll break your dirty little necks," McCollough

roared.

James yanked the shotgun loose from Kevin's hands. He sighted down the barrel at McCollough's head and pulled the trigger. The shotgun boomed, recoil digging into James' right shoulder. James lowered the barrel, centering point blank on the staggering figure's chest and pulled the trigger again. The muzzle flash blossomed in the darkness. The heavy concussion rolled out across the field. James centered again on McCollough's head and pulled the trigger a third time. The final impact turned the dead man halfway around. The gun was empty.

McCollough lay on his face, moving a single leg with dull repetition, like a broken toy. A wet gasping was all that issued from where his head had been. James handed the gun to Kevin, stiff-armed, and turned to continue toward the Hanging Tree.

Kevin stared dumbfounded at the receding figure of his cousin. Sam's mouth was a big "O" in the dimness. The remains of the old man crawled slowly about, the fierce wet sound of breathing coming from several places at once. The two boys hurried after James. As he ran, Kevin fished in his pocket and came up with his last four shells. He loaded three into the gun.

Mike struggled his way uphill in the pitch blackness of the brush and trees.

"Warren!" he yelled out.

"Get to the top!" Warren hollered back.

His panic rising, Mike redoubled his efforts to head uphill. The tangled underbrush clawed at his legs and arms.

"They're in here! They're in here with us!" Warren yelled.

Mike heard Warren's pistol fire. A bullet whined away through the underbrush. With the first muzzle flash, Mike saw the tracery of leaves and vines. With the second, he saw the shadows of leaves on his hands. With the third flash, he glimpsed the bulk of two dogs brushing against his legs. Something took hold of his right arm, pulling on it. Mike went down on his back. Someone was screaming. *Is that me?* Something else took hold of his pants leg. For a moment, he stopped struggling. He felt himself yanked to one side. A familiar feeling.

It's not fair, he thought, *being small.* Once he had been an equal, just another boy. Then as those around him grew quickly while he did not, a different life began, a life of feeding the egos of bigger boys. He hated the way boys he hardly knew leered at him across the locker room, crowded him, pushed him around. The way his friends left him behind for the weirdly agitated realm of chasing girls. The way he had become an appendage of the group, something tolerated. How his high-pitched shrieking laughter burst out of him when he was around them. *It's so unfair.* He began to thrash, fighting to pull free. He thought of Kevin outrunning him. Of his father's indifference. *All because of this weak stupid body.*

He kicked violently, feeling his shoe sink into something soft. He rolled onto his side and kicked again. The blow hit home and a foul puff of air blew into his face. The jaws holding his arm were rotted and weakened, its teeth failing to take purchase, popping loose. Mike pulled his arm free and rolled left, his hand found a rock as big as a soda can in the darkness.

He rose to his knees. A slick cold body brushed against him. Jaws raked along his ribs, snapping wildly. Mike swung hard with the stone in his right hand. The thing before him struggled sideways in the darkness. Mike took hold of it, oblivious to the rot and stench. He threw his weight on top of it, pushing it into the dirt. He found the head with his free hand, avoiding its clattering jaws, and began pounding with the stone. Then using both hands, he systematically pulverized the head.

He heard Warren yelling somewhere nearby. Mike crashed through the underbrush toward the sound of the voice. Bodies fell against him. One of the dogs was snapping about his legs. He struck wildly with the rock. He pushed forward, following Warren's voice. They found each other in the pitch blackness of the trees. Mike grabbed hold of the furry body that lunged clumsily about him in the blackness. He pinned its struggling cold form and pounded with the rock. With every blow, wild screams erupted from him, a string of vulgarity and rage. When he was sure the thing was badly enough damaged, he found Warren's arm in the darkness. They turned uphill, charging forward, holding firm to their grip on each other, unwilling to lose touch again in the inky darkness. When they broke through into the open, there before them was the barn and its outbuildings.

Mike was covered in gore, his right arm flecked with bone and flesh. Meaty clumps of fur clung to the stone in his hand. Warren stared at Mike. "Damn…" he said, reappraising the smaller boy. The moment passed. Warren hurriedly reloaded his pistol, dropping empty casings at his feet. Across the yard were the dogs, a half dozen or more.

"So much for leading them all away," Warren said.

"We're lucky *he's* not here," Mike said.

McCollough's dogs had decayed over the past day. Their movements were jerky and growing more uncontrolled. Some lay deflated in the grass. A few were standing.

"Move slowly," Warren whispered, clicking the reloaded pistol shut. He gingerly took a step forward and two more of the dogs rose to their feet. A gentle breeze stirred the limbs of the trees. The boys walked slowly across the yard. Mike glared at the dogs and spit. The dogs began moving about in small looping circles. Warren and Mike covered the last few yards to the barn door. Mike turned toward the dogs, now just a few yards away.

"AAAAAAAAA!" he screamed. "AAAAAAAAA!" He raised his arms and brandishing the bloody stone above his head. The dogs stopped their advance. Warren tried the barn door, yanking hard on the handle. The big, corrugated tin doors groaned but remained locked.

"You gotta go in the window," Warren said in a low voice. Mike backed up to where Warren was. The two boys stood beneath a bank of metal casement windows to the side of the double barn doors. Warren broke one of the panes of glass with the butt of his pistol. He reached inside and turned the latch. With some effort, the window swung out. Warren stuck the gun in its holster, couched down, and intertwined his fingers, motioning Mike to step up.

"You gonna give me the flashlight?" Mike said.

"No. I need it for the dogs. I don't think they like the light," Warren answered. "You got a match, right?"

"Yeah. I got a match. Man, this just gets better and better," Mike said. He stepped up and dragged himself struggling through the narrow window. After a moment of effort, he disappeared into the darkness of the barn.

Mike expected to fall several feet to the floor. Instead, he found himself on a long worktable. He fished in his pocket for one of the kitchen matches Warren had given him earlier. He struck it on the tabletop, and it flared to life. Outside, he heard Warren call out.

"It's a deadbolt, just turn it," Warren said.

Mike started to climb off the table and then stopped when he saw what was on the floor. He looked along the table toward the barn door. The worktable went all the way to the door.

"The place is full of snakes!" he shouted. He heard a gunshot outside. Crouching, he lit another match and shuffled down the length of the worktable, past tools, crates, and supplies to the doors. The match went out. He struck another and looked down. There were hundreds of snakes writhing in the dimness below.

One dog lurched forward. Warren raised the pistol and shot it in the head. It stared at him quizzically though the one good eye that was left. The others continued to circle, moving closer. The stench of rotting meat caused Warren to cover his mouth with his free hand. The animals wove back and forth. Warren put his back to the door.

"Mike," Warren said. "Open the door."

Still there was nothing.

"Mike," Warren repeated, his voice rising. The deadbolt turned with a loud click.

Warren yanked the door open. Mike stood pale and trembling on top of a five-gallon paint can. A carpet of snakes surged around the base of the can. Half rotten bodies rolled and tumbled, all moving like water on a beach, withdrawing and surging forward into the light.

"You know," Mike said, "Jimmy really ought to be here for this."

Chapter 13: Little Fires

James saw the Hanging Tree on the far side of the field, its dark form towering above the gray tree line beyond it. The field was silent. The boys jogged across the field. Before them, the tree rose, growing larger as they approached. As they crossed the last dozen yards the air seemed to thin. James felt a plucking sensation on his face and arms, like a static charge. Wisps of smoke still drifted up from the dark recesses beneath the tree's vast outstretched limbs.

He's here, James thought.

The darkness beneath the tree was impenetrable. There was no way to discern what was hidden there. James saw faint embers flare up in the blackness, as if something had bumped one of the charred logs McCollough had set on fire. Another ember jerked left and flared, was gone, and then reappeared, as if something had passed between it and James in the blackness.

James crouched down without taking his eyes off the tree. He began to pull up clumps of dry grass. He took a few wooden matches and held them between his teeth. He searched around in the darkness by his feet and found dry branches. One was a few feet long. He lit the grass and sticks and held the branch over the small flames.

"Get things to burn," he said to the others.

James felt wind rise from the direction of the tree. It was hot and stale. *Too late,* he thought. He stood slowly. The Hanged Man emerged from the blackness into the dim starlight.

It drifted forward. James raised the burning branch, throwing warm light across the ground about him. He put the small torch to the grass at his feet. Clumps of grass crackled and burned. James watched the pale figure of the Hanged Man as it came forward into the light.

James moved to one side. The Hanged Man turned with him. He stepped backwards. The Hanged Man came forward. James heard a whistling sound in his head, like a distant train coming, and then an immense force surged over him flowing out from the darkness under the branches.

James doubled over as suffocating sensations spilled into his head. The futile struggles of a thousand different lives ending, all within seconds. He felt flesh growing cold, the heat of his guts, dissipating. He felt a lifetime of the rhythmic undulations of life stuttering to a halt. There was screaming, tears, rage, denial, despair, suffocation, choking, and so much pain. He stumbled backwards and fell. There before him, his mother dangling in the air. Her lips were drawn back, mouthing silent curses. She fixed her eyes on him. Her hands contorted, twisting into warped unrecognizable shapes. Her spine twisted back on itself impossibly. Her feet, curved like horseshoes; flesh, but not flesh, snapping in half, splintering bone. She was screaming. It was absolute despair incarnate. She was tortured to break the boy's will. And it broke.

James screamed. He hurled the torch at the tree and ran, the Hanged Man close behind.

"It's following him," Sam said.

"Then he's done his part," Kevin replied. "Come on."

Kevin grabbed James' hastily made torch and moved toward the darkness beneath the tree. Light flickered from the grass fire that James had set. It sputtered from one clump of grass to the next. The torch burned weakly. Kevin turned it in his hand to ignite more of the branch. It grew brighter. He lay his shotgun on the ground. The two boys glanced toward where James had disappeared across the field.

"He's giving us time. Don't waste it," Kevin said.

The two boys dashed in beneath the great limbs of the tree and found the massive trunk. The temperature began to fall. The air grew foggy. Kevin's torch was burning up quickly. Sam threw down his armload of kindling at the base of the trunk. He grabbed charred logs, which lay in the shadows at his feet, pulling them toward the tree and laying them across the kindling. Kevin pushed his torch in beneath the pile of firewood.

A torrent of cold air blew out the torch plunging them into absolute darkness. Sam heard the limbs creaking rhythmically overhead. He turned and brushed against a cold musty body before him. It moved like meat on a hook. He turned again only to find his way blocked. He recoiled from the where his hand had touched the next body. "Kevin," he yelled.

Kevin heard Sam's cry faintly, as if over a great distance. He forced his way forward and banged his hand against the trunk. He sprang backwards in the darkness into a wall of bodies. He turned in a circle, feeling for a gap in the grisly cage that closed around him. A cold hard hand grabbed his hair. Another closed on his shoulder. Suddenly, all the bodies were moving and thrashing. He twisted and fell. He scrambled up and pushed forward again through the dangling wall. He screamed.

Mike stood before Warren balanced precariously on the paint can. At the smaller boy's feet writhed a sea of churning snakes, which ended exactly at the threshold of the doorway.

Warren put his pistol in Mike's hand and lifted him over the threshold into the yard. "I'm gonna get the kerosene cans. They're not far."

"You're going in there?" Mike whispered.

Warren pointed at his leather ranch boots. "Snakes can't get though them," he said. Then drawing a deep breath, Warren strode into the barn. As he moved forward in the darkness, he felt the patter of strikes against his boots. It sounded like rainfall.

He turned on his flashlight. Before him was a shelf. There were two cans on it. He took down the larger of the two and shook it. It was nearly full. He unscrewed the lid and sniffed it. Kerosene. There was a ceaseless hail of pattering against his boots.

Warren turned and shone his light across the darkness of the barn. Big gleaming metal flashed in the shadows.

Kevin was no longer beneath the limbs of the tree. Had he been pushed? He touched his chest. There was a cold spot. His sweat was icy cold. He looked up, confusion on his face. He could see nothing of the area under the limbs. A dense gray fog had gathered. He could hear Sam screaming, distant and muffled. Kevin rose and pushed his way tentatively into the fog beneath the tree. He felt a deep chill, as he entered. He could see nothing as the fog closed around him. He felt something push him. Hands tore at him, Sam was screaming, and then Kevin again fell out from beneath the tree onto the ground; exactly as he had been before.

"Sam!" he yelled, rising. He heard nothing. "Sam!" he

repeated. He charged forward again into the cold darkness beneath the tree.

Mike stood with his back to the interior of the barn. The dogs were close now.

"Warren?" Mike said. "We gotta go!"

He heard a metal clank from inside the barn. He turned and glanced back toward Warren's flashlight beam.

"Warren?" he said.

Light suddenly poured out of the barn. Mike spun to face a bank of floodlights blazing before him, as an engine roared to life. Mike pushed both barn doors open. A big blue ranch tractor emerged into the yard.

The dogs scattered, limping, and crawling to avoid the blinding light that poured off floodlights mounted above the cab.

"Get on!" Warren yelled.

Mike clambered up onto the cab and stood behind the chair. He breathed in the rattling diesel exhaust like it was the smell of Sunday chicken dinner. He set his feet on the big differential and held on to the superstructure.

"Dad said Hagel was storing equipment. He didn't say it was a tractor!" Warren yelled. Grinning, he pointed toward the attachment mounted on the back of the tractor, held off the ground by a set of hydraulics.

"A bush whacker!" Warren yelled.

"What's it do?" Mike hollered back.

Warren leaned down, felt around for a moment, and found what he was looking for. He put the transmission in reverse and backed the tractor up, positioning the bush whacker over the snakes roiling just inside the barn doors. They swarmed impotently three to four feet below, many already crushed by the big wheels. Warren threw a lever and the engine's RPMs lagged as big mowing blades spun to life beneath the cover of the bush whacker. Then he dropped the mower onto the snakes. Red spray covered the dirt of the yard.

Laughing hysterically, the two boys gave each other a high five. Warren raised the spraying bush whacker and shoved the tractor into forward gear. He wedged the red metal gas can beneath his seat and prepared to let out the clutch.

"Hold on, tight!" Warren yelled. He lifted his leg the full length of the long clutch stroke and the tractor lurched forward. He opened the throttle and wheeled into the yard. The tractor bounced along, turning to head out the open gate towards the Hanging Tree, a shaft of blinding illumination shining out fifty feet ahead of it.

Kevin forced his way deeper into the chilling darkness beneath the tree. This time, he drove forward with his shoulder, pumping his legs fiercely like a running back. The dark coldness enveloped him. Thick heavy objects hung, blocking his way, closing in behind him.

"Sam!" he yelled. A hand clawed the side of his face. He lashed out to the right, feeling his forearm sink into something. He threw himself forward again, ducking lower in the blackness. He realized he was driving his way through human bodies, but he pushed the thought aside. Something repulsive brushed against his face. His arms and legs thrashed, but his sense of direction was faltering.

"Sam!" he yelled again. He felt his feet slip from beneath him. He fell to his knees and rose upward, lashing out, hammering his elbows brutally against the shapes around him. He advanced slowly, gaining only inches. The blows against his body seemed to grow more targeted. Cold, hard knuckled fists crashed against his head. His movements grew weaker. He fell to his knees and covered his head with his arms. Dangling feet kicked at him wildly; careening blows off his ribs and his head.

"Help me!" Sam yelled faintly.

Kevin sucked in air and rose, pushing forward, his leg muscles burning. Knuckles skidded off his cheek, stinging fiercely. He grabbed a fist and reached up it to find the cold damp bulk on his right. He threw his arms about the stinking mass and yanked down with all his strength. He felt the neck, somewhere in the darkness above, tear and give way.

He yelled as the body fell past him to the ground. He pushed on toward Sam's faint voice, lashing out at everything about him, shoving bodies aside, fighting for room to go forward. His chest was running with sweat. He was a flame of life in a sea of dead things.

"Kevin!" Sam screamed now directly before him. Kevin found Sam's shirt collar and dragging him up, threw his arms around him. Kevin covered his head amidst the hail of violent blows. A fist drove into his forehead. Another cracked against his cheek. Half a dozen violent blows fell in the time it took to get Sam to his feet. Holding Sam, Kevin lunged forward into the gauntlet of thrashing dangling bodies, pushing and shoving with his free arm and shoulder. Sam began to push as well, struggling to get his numb legs to move. Kevin's hands slipped on Sam's torso, damp with blood and sweat.

"I can't see," Sam yelled.

"Just push, you asshole," Kevin yelled. He grabbed Sam's neck in a half nelson and shouted into his ear. "Push!"

He felt Sam's legs begin to pump frantically, driving the two of them onward. They held tightly to each other, yelling in the blackness. And then it ended. They fell forward into the open air, gasping.

Kevin climbed to his feet and collapsed again; his legs too weak to support him. His hair was plastered to his face and neck. Out from underneath the tree, it seemed like daylight compared to the darkness within.

Sam crawled away and collapsed. He touched his face. It was numb. A ringing filled his ears. He raised his head and saw the last vestiges of the grass fire flickering before him. He rose and stumbled over to it, tearing up loose grass and adding it to the flames. He struggled to remain upright and gather more flammable material as the flames rose higher. Kevin appeared next to him holding his shotgun. They looked at each other, shocked and utterly beyond words.

Chapter 14: The Trap

James ran for his life through the midnight fields. Bull nettle and cactus thrashed at his legs. A fierce buzzing filled his ears, drowning out the pounding of his feet against the hard packed earth. Behind him, the Hanged Man followed close at his heels. In a panic, James turned toward the tree line, lunging in among the trees, seeking to escape. The long night had taken a brutal toll on him. Whispering voices rose in the woods about him as he clawed his way forward, desperate to leave the Hanged Man behind. Suddenly, he found himself in a circular clearing about thirty yards across. Starlight lit the open ground. James bent over, struggling to get his wind back. He saw pale figures emerging from among the trees.

The dead were converging on him. No longer aimless, the spirits were collecting around him, reaching, grasping for him. They grew more solid, forcing James toward the center of the clearing. Before him, the remains of an old, stacked stone fireplace was all that was left of a long-forgotten homestead.

He turned to see the Hanged Man at the edge of the grove. It drifted in place, its face obscured in the shadows of the tree limbs that bordered the grove. At the edge of the trees, James saw the faces of the dead now still, staring back, their eyes reflecting the starlight.

But the trees were changing, growing unnaturally quickly. Dim branches lengthened and twisted before his eyes. Curling and cracking, they exploded in an unnatural blanket of new growth, snaking forth, elongating. The figures of the dead, still staring, were blotted out by a riot of coiling branches. James looked for a way to get out the clearing, but the wall of growth was now impenetrable on all sides.

The Hanged Man crossed into the grove. The branches twisted closed behind it, squealing and snapping. The air was full of rustling as the wall of limbs pushed in toward the center of the grove.

"This isn't real," James whispered. He stepped to the wall of grey branches and put out his hand. The limbs were solid, twisting and turning beneath his palm. "No," he said, backing away from the hard unnatural writhing.

The Hanged Man lurched towards him. He ducked away, dropping to his hands and knees, dashing aside on all fours. *I'm trapped.* He wiped the sweat from his face. He stood only to feel himself pushed by the coiling branches behind him. The circle was closing very quickly. He stepped toward the Hanged Man and again felt the stabbing touch of the twisting tree limbs behind him.

The Hanged Man's cold white hands, bound at its waist, were clenching and unclenching. James looked up at its shadowy face. Exhausted, the boy felt a sense of acceptance stealing over him. *Making me give up,* James thought. He tried to shake off the lazy calm, but it returned. He felt the twisting growing limbs push stiff fingers into his back, nudging him to within inches of the Hanged Man.

"Somebody help me!" he yelled. The cry trailed off into the trees. The eerie silence brought all his terror rushing to the surface. The Hanged Man's hands reached for him.

The wall of limbs shoved him forward one final step. There was no room. He pressed himself back. James heard a fluttering. He glanced to the side and saw that a red cardinal had settled on his shoulder; its black eyes looking into his. James pictured the figure he had seen moving sinuously in the candlelight.

"Please. Help me... " he whispered. It was a brief final prayer.

The bird cocked his head. "And there it is," a woman's voice said somewhere behind him. '

The Hanged Man struck him, its hard cold fingers raking along the side of James' head. He tumbled to the dirt, stars flashing before his eyes, his ears ringing. He raised his head and saw the cardinal's dim form leaping on the ground before him, its wings spread, a bright red flag in the dimness.

James reached out. His hand disappeared up to his elbow in a small opening in the ground, no bigger than his fist. Something cold and hard brushed his shoulder. He pushed his other hand into the hole. Clods of dirt gave way like paper. A dark damp cave opened. He pitched headlong downward into the earth itself.

Kevin and Sam heard the tractor coming across the field. They had been working to get a small fire going just a foot or two away from the ring of the Hanging Tree's branches. The loud clatter of the diesel engine echoed through the darkness. Light flashed on the hillside and then flared again. Pillars of white light spread among the trees. The tractor appeared, bouncing out onto the flat open field. It wheeled and came toward them. Then they heard Mike's high-pitched screaming.

"Yes! Yes! Yes!" he kept yelling as the tractor bore down on them. Sam began jumping up and down, waving his arms. The tractor rolled up and shuddered to a halt with its floodlights shining in toward the tree. Very little could be seen beneath the great limbs. The tractor's white floodlight beams were scattered by the dark gray fog. Vague shapes moved in the dimness. A wind began to rise. Mike leapt down and ran toward Kevin and Sam with the red gas can.

"It's kerosene!" he yelled, holding it up clumsily in both hands. The fire the boys had built was flaring in the wind, throwing harsh shadows on their faces. Lightning exploded across the sky. Kevin grabbed the kerosene and handed it to Sam. Then Kevin ran to the tractor to help Warren.

Warren opened a big metal toolbox mounted on the back of the tractor and took out a pair of work gloves. He pulled them on and lifted the lid again. "Where's James?" he yelled.

"He ran. It followed him," Kevin answered over the drone of the tractor engine. He pointed to show where James had disappeared. Then he jerked his thumb toward the tree "We can't get in under the tree! There's something in there! They attacked us! We can't get close enough to set the fire!" Kevin's hair was matted with blood.

Warren pulled the end of a long thick length of chain out of the box. "Help me get this to the tree!" he said. The chain had a thick "S" shaped hook on the end of it. Warren jogged away toward the tree dragging the chain. It coiled out of the metal box with a deafening rattle. Following, Kevin handed his shotgun to Sam, took hold of the chain, and pulled as well. The wind rose higher, buffeting the boys, threatening to blow out the fire.

Warren paused at the edge of the tree's overhang. He peered into the swirling darkness beneath its limbs. The floodlights from the tractor lit him brightly but he could see nothing beneath the limbs. Something rushed forward out of the dimness, drew to a halt, and then receded into the darkness again. Warren's lips pulled back in an involuntary grimace.

"Goddamn tree," he said under his breath.

Warren dropped the chain at his feet. Lightning flashed again. He ran back to the tractor's storage box. He found a thick orange extension cord. He returned to the tree. Holding the free end of the cord in his hand, he flung the other end over a long thick branch above him. Quickly he tied the end of the chain to the extension cord and pulled the chain up over the branch and back down to the ground. He flung the cord over again. In minutes he had the chain wrapped three times around the branch. Kevin reached up as high as he could and hooked the chain to itself. They ran back towards the tractor and Warren put the other end of the chain in Kevin's hands.

"I'm turning the tractor around!" Warren yelled. Rain began to pelt the ground. Soon it was falling heavily. Warren climbed onto the seat and turned the tractor in a quick loop so that it backed up to the tree. The rain thundered down, falling in sheets past the headlights. Warren climbed down and helped Kevin secure the free end of the chain to the hitch on the back of the tractor. The big chain dangled off the upright mower assembly.

"The fire's gone!" Sam yelled over the storm. The boys glanced toward the smoldering pile of branches then went back to working.

"I can't drive straight away from the tree!" Warren yelled, pulling Kevin aside. "The chain will slide off. I'm going to go away at an angle."

A deafening bang echoed across the field. The tractor's back end was dragged toward the tree. The chain had been yanked taught, disappearing into the darkness surrounding the trunk. There was a loud groan. The tractor slid another foot toward the tree, the heavy chain ringing like a piano wire, near the breaking point.

"Jesus Christ!" Mike yelled. "It's taking the tractor!"

"The hell it is," Warren yelled. He climbed back onto the driver's seat. With a howl of straining metal, the tractor was yanked another foot closer to the tree. Warren fell sideways, hanging on by the steering wheel. He pulled himself into the seat and shoved the tractor into gear. He turned the wheel and stomped on the gas. The motor roared, belching black smoke. With a clank, the transmission engaged and the big rear wheels ground forward. The tractor bucked. Its front wheels rose off the ground and then fell back. The chain held taught. Warren shifted to a lower gear and accelerated again. The front end bucked again, and the motor bogged down.

Thunder rumbled and lightning flashed. Lightning arced down from the storming sky, striking among the trees nearby. Through the rain, the boys saw a tree explode in a shower of sparks. Chunks of burning limbs spun through the rain to land in fiery heaps. Kevin pointed to the gas can and hollered at Sam.

"Spread it on the ground as close under the tree as you can get," he yelled. Then he took off running toward the nearest burning limb a dozen yards away. He slipped once and fell but was back on his feet and running in seconds. He reached the blazing remains of a gnarled tree limb. Flames roared skyward off it despite the falling rain. It had flown hundreds of feet through the air and then left a long trench where it landed in the hard dirt of the field. Kevin grabbed the end that wasn't in flames, hefted it in his arms, and ran back with it.

Warren watched in horror as the chain yanked the tractor closer and closer. He felt the transmission shuddering beneath him. The tractor felt like it was shaking apart. It would soon be pulled in beneath the tree.

"You can't pull a damn tractor," he yelled. He saw lightning strike again on the hill. He engaged the clutch, cursing, and revved the engine. He dumped the clutch; the back wheels began spinning. The shuddering tractor thrashed about on the wet ground.

Sam and Mike frantically gathered loose kindling and branches and made a pile close under the edge of the tree's drip line. Then they poured kerosene across it. Kevin came running back toward him through the rain. He flung the burning branch down on the pile of kerosene-soaked kindling and Sam poured another stream of kerosene across it all. Flames erupted, whipping up through the branches of the Hanging Tree.

"More!" Kevin yelled over the storm.

He grabbed the can from Sam and turned it upside down for long seconds. A single ball of fire and black smoke swept upward into the dense whipping foliage. A loud crackling and popping erupted as the flames flashed through the upper reaches of the tree.

Warren felt the chain go limp. The tractor leapt forward. Throwing the wheel left, he ground his foot down hard on the accelerator. The tractor wheeled and roared away. The chain, snaked along behind, ran out of length, and rose off the ground to snap taught around the limb above. The limb bent hard over and the wheels on the tractor began to slip. Warren swung the steering wheel further left, revving the engine. He plunged in for a moment under the branches. The exhaust pipe on the tractor was bent sideways, the big wheels churning the mud.

Then the branch shuddered, and deep in near the trunk, cracked, and gave way. The tractor leapt forward, and Warren turned out from under the tree. Behind the tractor trailed the big dark tree limb. It was as thick as an oil drum at its base and revealed a long white expanse of heart wood. A whole section of the tree's trunk was carved out. Immediately the rain slacked off, like a spigot being shut off. Now only the thunder rolled overhead. Warren swung the tractor around and turning, caught the others in the bright beam of the headlights.

They rushed toward Warren cheering as lightning struck the tractor.

Chapter 15: Open the Door

James rolled and fell, tumbling downward before he came to a halt in the darkness. He was in a cave of some kind or a tunnel. Thin roots dangled along his neck. He raised his hand above his head and felt moist dirt and something else, earthworms moving frantic and blind. He brought his hand quickly down. He could hear other movements about him in the darkness. Slowly, a flickering light rose somewhere ahead of him. The tunnel before him was alive with insects of all kinds, crawling in frantic haste about the walls and floors. The weak light filtered down the tunnel from somewhere ahead.

He started forward along the narrow passage on his hands and knees. Insects dropped down on his neck. He brushed them off. He placed his hand down on something hard and metal. He raised the rusted remains of a large bore pistol. He stared at it a moment and then dropped it, crawling on.

Blood ran down his cheek falling on the floor of the tunnel. He saw beetles wriggling in the red drops. He felt the prick of tiny sharp limbs against his palms. There was no place to crawl that was not covered in wriggling life. The bugs surged up in a wave before him, nearly as high as his elbows. He tried to back up but there was no tunnel behind him, just a solid dirt wall. He started forward again, the skin around his eye twitching. He pushed forward through the undulating wave of insects. They surged up his arms, surrounded his throat, crawled across his face and into his mouth. Then, suddenly, the surge of insects was gone.

A larger chamber opened before him. His hand encountered something amidst the carpet of wriggling insects. It was the head of a porcelain doll. Next to it was a woman's shoe with buttons, past that, a decaying skirt. Jewelry. A bracelet. There was a comb. His hand settled on a bone. He picked it up and turned it over in his hands. It was as long as his forearm. The next place he put his hand, the dirt gave way and his fingers slipped down between two ribs. He pulled his fingers free.

The light ahead was growing warmer and brighter. He saw a single candle burning. His vision blurred. Something moved next to the candle, only a smudged half visible shape. He blinked and looked down at his hands. They were clear and distinct. He looked up, struggling to focus, staring at the glowing smudge of candle flame. The air was rich with the smell of decay and loamy earth. Strange bulky shadows wriggled across the wall. He heard loud birdsong. Abruptly the small muddy chamber came into focus.

James saw a small wooden door, made of simple wooden planks, set into the clay and rock wall before him. Bugs swarmed along its face. He crawled toward it, running his hands across its rough surface. Partway up, there was a small patch of leather held in place by a battered nail. Lower down was a dark leather strap that served as a doorknob. James placed his fingers against the smaller patch of leather and pushed it aside. A brilliant shaft of sunlight streamed into the chamber.

Someone spoke.

"I come down here to hide when strangers are about,"

she said. James turned to see the woman from the house. She lay propped up against the dirt wall, her dress, as before, was torn open to reveal a gaping red wound between her breasts. Her head hung limp. Her eyes were staring. Her hands were open and upturned at her sides. A rifle lay across her lap. She lay exactly as he had seen her before.

A bright red cardinal perched on her shoulder, picking at her hair. It eyed him, its head cocked sideways. Then, a hundred of the bright red birds clung all over her, their wings flapping, blocking her from sight. Then none. A beetle tumbled down across her shoulder, kicking, and struggling. She was perfectly still, her voice low, hardly audible. There were no longer any insects at all in the small chamber.

"The violence that some men do. Do they not see how it creates such terrible echoes in the world?"

Her long blonde hair glowed in the light of the candle. A patch fell out, tumbling down her chest, revealing a section of shattered skull and something black. Snakes wriggled out from beneath her hands and disappeared beneath her skirt. Again, a bird was singing. The sound was muted and distant. A cardinal appeared hopping in the dirt at her feet. The rifle became water, running down between her legs, making pools of mud on the floor of the chamber.

"Two men came and found me out in the field. They chased me down and beat me. They raped me. Then, they shot me. It was such a hot day, I crawled back to the house. It was too hot to die out there." The whispering voice was so very faint.

She was gone. The chamber was instantly swarming again with insects. They fluttered about the candle and swarmed along the floor and walls. James turned back to the little door. He tried pulling on the leather strap. The door did not give. James pulled harder. The leather tore through.

James lifted the little scrap of leather covering the peephole and put his eye to it. He saw the house by the well, sunlight streaming down. He heard a creaking on the porch just out of his line of sight, a rocking chair. He rubbed his eyes and looked again.

"Your friends are going to die," the woman said. Again, she sat propped against the wall. James stared at her.

"Too bad, you're not strong enough," she continued. "That's too bad. We had such high hopes for you. But you're too weak," The pale white lips drew back off her teeth.

"What are you?" James said.

"What the fuck are you?" she replied, snarling. A wet gurgling rose in her throat. A pink bubble of blood burst against her lips staining them red.

"Open the door," she said.

James turned to the door. The handle was there again. Intact. He slipped his fingers along the edge of the door and strained against it. The boards did not give.

"It's locked," he said.

"Your friends are gonna die, right *now*," she wheezed. Blood ran down her chest. The room was empty. Bugs surged back and forth across the floor.

James set his hands along the edge of the door and pulled wildly, thrashing about in the small space. The candle sputtered, threatening to plunge the room into darkness.

A very different voice spoke as the darkness encroached. "Gonna break your little necks," something behind him said. The candle became brighter again. James was in the corner. His hands up, his eyes rolling back into his head. He pushed his way back up to the door. The candle sputtered again, failing. He knew that there was no more time.

Like the last second before being found in hide and seek. He faced the door. He placed his hand in the strap. Something big began to move about in the room behind him. He stared at the door, exerting no force against it. The candle was knocked over. Darkness descended. *Now*, he thought, and pushing the door open, he stepped out into the yard before the sunlit porch.

The woman from the house sat in a chair rocking slowly back and forth. She held no rifle. She was not wounded. Her eyes were unusually blue.

"I have always admired ingenuity," she said, showing no expression.

James felt dizzy. Waves of exhaustion swept over him. She looked away.

"I will admit he beat me, but he never did more than blacken my eye or bruise me up. Well within his rights... well within his rights..." She stared off across the open fields, her face slack and expressionless.

"I can barely stay awake....," James murmured. He dropped down to his knees and then sat heavily.

"But he was known to be an ill-tempered man and they thought he had murdered me. So they hung him – twice, as I recall," she said.

James heard something scrambling frantically about in the house.

"Call him now and we will put an end to it, finally," she said.

"I don't know his name," James replied, his speech slurring heavily.

She spoke a name, but he could not hear it. The empty wind whispered across his ears. He shrugged his shoulders and frowned up at her.

"His name is..." she said it again. Her lips moved but there was no name.

She looked at him for a moment. A deep sadness crossed her features. Then, rising, she took a long hairpin from her hair. She walked to the edge of the porch and reached out for James' hand. She took his wrist and stared into his eyes, birdsong. Her touch was like the movement of the insects, squirming.

"For this thing, I am deeply sorry," she said.

Then she pushed the pin through his right hand.

"Roy Redman," she said in a calm level voice.

"Roy Redman," the boy said, lightning skittering silently along the edges of his vision. The sounds in the house became more pronounced. Something crashed to the floor. The sky grew dark.

"Won't you please direct him to me here," she said. A flicker. She was back, sitting again. Her face blurred, the sky grew pitch black, shafts of sunlight danced on the porch, birdsong rose hissing and chaotic.

James turned and stepped drunkenly away from the porch. He had trouble breathing. The air was thin and slippery, unable to fill him. Flares of light traced the edges of the trees as their branches tossed in utter silence against the blackening sky. Flashbulb lights among the trees exploded, leaving a haze of white, followed by the details of the trees fading back into view.

James turned to look back at the woman on the porch. As he turned, he saw the view of the trees before him rotate with him. Again, he tried to turn toward her, but the house remained beyond his line of sight. He walked onward away from the house. On his left, he saw the cistern, the outline of a low retaining wall. He turned toward it, putting his right hand out against its cold face to steady himself.

"I'm killed now too, Momma," he murmured.

He peered down through the haze before his eyes and saw the hairpin that ran through his right hand. It was shiny and silver, with a cluster of cloisonné flowers embellishing the top of the shaft. He reached for it with his left hand and found himself tipping over into the well.

James pushed up out of the hot earth, gasping for air. Clumps of soil clung to his fingers and hair. He shook his head and struggled out of the damp hole. Wiping his filthy sleeve across his lips, he began laughing, a high unnatural tittering.

Chapter 16: Lanterns

The boys saw the lightning trace its way down and lick the superstructure of the tractor. There was a white flash and a rush of hot air. The concussion knocked them off their feet.

Warren was thrown skyward. He saw the black bulk of the Hanging Tree roll past before the ground came up to strike him. He felt the bones in his leg give way. He rolled twice and came to a halt twenty feet from the tractor. He saw the last of the raindrops falling toward him out of the dark sky. They glowed orange, lit by the burning tractor as they fell wavering down from above. He blinked. The ground beneath him was as hard as stone, holding him flat. He smelled bacon cooking. No, it wasn't bacon. Almost as an afterthought, he took a breath.

Kevin was the first to reach him. Warren tried to sit up. Kevin pushed him down.

"Stay down. I think your leg is broken," Kevin said to him. Warren fell back, staring up, a puzzled look on his face. He was taking in small breaths of air over and over. Sam and Mike were peering over Kevin's shoulder. Mike looked about and patted Kevin on the arm.

"It's coming back," Mike said.

There in the distance, the Hanged Man rushed towards them, swept along like a tattered white flag in the wind.

Kevin looked toward the tree. Parts of the burning tractor had spun in underneath and were clearly visible burning there. He shoved the gas can into Sam's hands and took up his shotgun.

"Burn it," Kevin said, and he turned to face the monster. He searched his pockets. He found a final loose shotgun shell. He flipped the shotgun over and tried to insert the shell. It only went in halfway and then stopped. That meant there were three shells in the gun already. He pushed the shell into his front pocket. The Hanged Man emerged out of the dimness, fully lit by the burning tractor. The Hanged Man's head jerked about spasmodically, its neck like a thick serpent, twitching and convulsing, a sack of hard muscle over broken bone.

The long night of running had left Kevin exhausted. He was falling victim to pain, shock, and deep confusion. He flipped off the safety on the shotgun and started walking forward.

The Hanged Man swept up before him. Kevin raised the shotgun and fired point blank directly into its face, to no effect. Nothing.

"No! Not this way," he shouted, turning the shotgun in his hands, and swinging it with all his might. The gun's stock thumped against the gray expanse of the Hanged Man's shoulder. The dusty shirt split from the impact. Back peddling, Kevin swung the stock hard across the side of the monster's head and again, more violently, down across its collarbone. The gun spun loose from his hands and fell to the ground to be swallowed by the shadows among the high grass.

The monster collided with him, knocking Kevin onto his back. He rose immediately and flung himself toward where the shotgun had fallen into the shadows. He raked his hands across the ground, seeking the gun. A blow stuck him behind his ear and pitched him forward on his face. Hard hands grabbed him as he struggled to rise. He was yanked into the air. The dim ground spun drunkenly below him. One hand had him by his hair. Another took hold of him by his ear. He dangled for a moment, kicking wildly. Then a hand found his throat, turning his head up. Kevin saw the Hanged Man's dark face lit by a momentary flash halo. He heard the boom of the twenty gauge and felt the ground hit him hard. He rose, struggling to stand.

Mike stood holding the shotgun, his eyes wide. The Hanged Man swept toward him. The smaller boy was knocked over backwards. Then the creature turned away from them. Someone was coming towards them out of the darkness. And he was laughing.

Sam glanced towards the tree and then back to his friends hurrying away. He took the gas can and darted in under the limbs of the great tree. Ahead, he saw two bright fires, plastic and rubber pieces of the tractor burning fiercely. Something new was visible just beyond the fire, near the trunk of the tree.

There was a small, bloated figure there. It lay against the base of tree, its body pale and oily. It seemed to shift and waver as he looked at it. It swept its arms up once and the chill descended. Sam poured kerosene on the nearest fire. A ball of fire swept up through the limbs of the tree.

In the flood of light, Sam saw the figure struggle, like a slug on hot pavement. A pink tongue licked out from its face. The thing lolled against the tree trunk, too gorged, and bloated to rise. Malevolent red eyes burned like hot pin holes in its vague face. The pink tongue flickered. It waved its arms wildly. Sam heard the tree begin to shuffle and shift above him. He stepped around the first fire and flung kerosene along the trunk of the tree. It splashed across the figure on the ground.

The thing's voice was a wet whisper directly in Sam's ear, unintelligible. Sam slapped at his ear, horrified. There was a grinding sound. An immense limb crashed to the ground next to Sam, slashing him brutally across his back. He rose and turned the can upside down pouring kerosene across the trunk of the tree, a puddle pooling at its base. Backing away, he poured the last of the kerosene in a trail along the ground, emptying the can as he backed up to a second fire nearby.

Fire leapt along the trail of kerosene to engulf the thing beneath the tree. Flames leapt up the trunk, rising into the limbs. Sam dropped the can and ran.

James was now silent, standing before the Hanged Man. He and the monster were motionless, as if a battle of wills was taking place somewhere far out of sight. Kevin started forward, but James held up his hand. *Wait.*

The monster drifted gently forward and took the boy by his throat lifting him up off the ground. James continued to hold his palm out to the boys. Then, without any sign of distress, he raised his right hand and with his left, drew a long silver pin from it. The pin slid out slowly as the two figures turned gently in the air. James was choking to death, but he didn't seem to care. After an agonizingly long time, the pin slid free of his hand and James pushed it gently into the chest of the Hanged Man. He whispered something they could not hear. The pin slid in without resistance up to the colored decorations on its end and the monster dropped James to the ground.

James lay where he fell, unmoving. The Hanged Man began to shrivel and crack, warping, with puffs of dust rising into the air. A high keening rose, as if the thing was being torn apart from within.

Kevin rushed forward, shoved the shotgun into the Hanged Man's face and pulled the trigger. The blast blew the creature's head into a dozen chunks that rained down for yards beyond. The Hanged Man turned and swept toward him, its jaw hanging loose, wagging fitfully. Kevin pulled the trigger again, but the gun was empty. He spun it around in his hands and gripping the barrel, clubbed the Hanged Man across its neck tearing it open.

Kevin stood his ground over James who lay broken in the dirt. Lightning flashed. The boy's lips were pulled back off his teeth as he swung the heavy shotgun again and again. Bits of the wooden stock splintered and spun off into the air. He felt the brittle bones of the thing shattering and giving way.

The Hanged Man tipped back under the assault. Kevin turned the shotgun in his hands and taking the last shell from his pocket pushed it into the breech. He flipped the gun over.

The Hanged Man shook. The remains of its head rotated wildly. Its shoulders and chest were battered out of shape. It was falling to pieces. And still it came at him. Kevin leveled the shotgun at its gut and fired. The monster swept past. Kevin saw it turning. He turned with it.

No further attack came. The creature was caught up in a violent flurry of motion. Kevin's final shot had cut through the leather strips that had bound its wrists. The Hanged Man's arms were free. It spun like a whirling dervish, its arms helicoptering about it so uncontrollably that it was beating the remains of its skull to pieces.

Kevin saw fire rising in a glowing rush through the Hanging Tree in the distance. Flames filled the limbs of the old oak. It glowed like a vast lantern, lighting the field for hundreds of feet in all directions.

The Hanged Man's violent gyrations slowed. It drifted,

facing the burning tree which was engulfed in flames. Sparks rose a hundred feet into the sky. The Hanged Man moved in slow circles across the field, dancing a stately pirouette as flames leapt higher into the night sky. Flames appeared along its legs. They spurted from its fingertips and blazed to life from deep in its chest. It continued to turn slowly, gracefully as the flames consumed it. Then, like flash paper, it was gone, a final flurry of sparks rising into the night sky.

Kevin and Mike helped James to his feet. He was unaware of them; a long gush of saliva rolled down his chin. The boys each took him by the arm and led him back to the others.

From the direction of town, they heard sirens.

About the Author

Mark Greene was born and raised in Texas. He lives in New York City with his wife and son. This is his first work of fiction. A follow up to Dance of the Hanged Man will be published in 2024. It is titled Ghost Light.

***

Like our book? We're a *very* small publisher. If you would like to help us share Dance of the Hanged Man with new readers, please consider:

1) ...sharing a photo of your copy of our book and your thoughts on social media. You can tag us on most platforms @RemakingManhood
2) ...leaving a review on our book's Amazon page.
3) ...telling your friends!

For small publishers like us, these three actions are a powerful boost. It literally makes writing the next book possible. So, thank you, <u>sincerely.</u>

You can find us at ThinkPlayPartners.com.
We look forward to hearing from you.